THE QUEEN WINS

The Count, without saying a word, lifted Tarena onto the side saddle of the horse she was to ride and then mounted himself on the other one, saying to the groom,

"Be waiting here in an hour when we will return."

The groom touched his forelock and they rode off with the Count leading the way.

He took her through the trees at the back of the Palace into a field that led to open land behind the City.

When they reached it, Tarena knew instinctively what he intended to do.

She pressed her stallion forward into a gallop and the Count did the same and then they were riding over long grass and butterflies and birds rose up in front of them.

It was some time before the Count pulled in his horse.

When Tarena looked round, she found they were quite a long way from the City. In fact she could only just see the roof of the Palace and little else.

"That was lovely!" she breathed.

"I thought it was a diversion you really needed," said the Count.

Now their two stallions were walking quietly side by side and then suddenly Tarena exploded,

"He is *horrible!* He is *beastly!* I cannot marry him!"

The words seemed to burst through her lips and for a moment she broke the beauty and the quiet around them.

THE BARBARA CARTLAND PINK COLLECTION

Titles in this series

THE QUEEN WINS

BARBARA CARTLAND

Barbaracartland.com Ltd

THE BARBARA CARTLAND PINK COLLECTION

Dame Barbara Cartland is still regarded as the most prolific bestselling author in the history of the world.

In her lifetime she was frequently in the Guinness Book of Records for writing more books than any other living author.

Her most amazing literary feat was to double her output from 10 books a year to over 20 books a year when she was 77 to meet the huge demand.

She went on writing continuously at this rate for 20 years and wrote her very last book at the age of 97, thus completing an incredible 400 books between the ages of 77 and 97.

Her publishers finally could not keep up with this phenomenal output, so at her death in 2000 she left behind an amazing 160 unpublished manuscripts, something that no other author has ever achieved.

Barbara's son, Ian McCorquodale, together with his daughter Iona, felt that it was their sacred duty to publish all these titles for Barbara's millions of admirers all over the world who so love her wonderful romances.

So in 2004 they started publishing the 160 brand new Barbara Cartlands as *The Barbara Cartland Pink Collection*, as Barbara's favourite colour was always pink – and yet more pink!

The Barbara Cartland Pink Collection is published monthly exclusively by Barbaracartland.com and the books are numbered in sequence from 1 to 160.

Enjoy receiving a brand new Barbara Cartland book each month by taking out an annual subscription to the Pink Collection, or purchase the books individually.

The Pink Collection is available from the Barbara Cartland website www.barbaracartland.com via mail order and through all good bookshops.

In addition Ian and Iona are proud to announce that The Barbara Cartland Pink Collection is now available in ebook format as from Valentine's Day 2011.

For more information, please contact us at:

Barbaracartland.com Ltd.
Camfield Place
Hatfield
Hertfordshire AL9 6JE
United Kingdom

Telephone: +44 (0)1707 642629
Fax: +44 (0)1707 663041
Email: info@barbaracartland.com

THE LATE DAME BARBARA CARTLAND

Barbara Cartland who sadly died in May 2000 at the age of nearly 99 was the world's most famous romantic novelist who wrote 723 books in her lifetime with worldwide sales of over 1 billion copies and her books were translated into 36 different languages.

As well as romantic novels, she wrote historical biographies, 6 autobiographies, theatrical plays, books of advice on life, love, vitamins and cookery. She also found time to be a political speaker and television and radio personality.

She wrote her first book at the age of 21 and this was called *Jigsaw*. It became an immediate bestseller and sold 100,000 copies in hardback and was translated into 6 different languages. She wrote continuously throughout her life, writing bestsellers for an astonishing 76 years. Her books have always been immensely popular in the United States, where in 1976 her current books were at numbers 1 & 2 in the B. Dalton bestsellers list, a feat never achieved before or since by any author.

Barbara Cartland became a legend in her own lifetime and will be best remembered for her wonderful romantic novels, so loved by her millions of readers throughout the world.

Her books will always be treasured for their moral message, her pure and innocent heroines, her good looking and dashing heroes and above all her belief that the power of love is more important than anything else in everyone's life.

"You will know the old saying, 'better to have loved and lost than to have never loved at all', and when I am asked if I agree, I say, 'Yes I do, because you will always treasure your memories of love in your heart for ever'."

Barbara Cartland

CHAPTER ONE
1887

Tarena walked round the garden thinking just how lovely the flowers were and how much she loved living in the pretty little Vicarage in Oxfordshire.

She knew how pleased her uncle would be to see the flamboyant blooms when he returned from the North.

She was sure, as the weather had been bad, that he would have found few flowers to enjoy in Northumberland and so he would be thrilled to be back in Oxfordshire again where the sun was shining brightly.

She wondered if his father, the Earl of Grandbrooke was still alive and she was expecting a letter from him later in the day telling her the latest news.

The Honourable the Reverend Richard Brooke was the younger son of the tenth Earl of Grandbrooke.

As was traditional his elder brother had gone into the Army and Richard was promised one of the Parishes on the great estate belonging to his father.

First he had studied at Oxford to obtain his degree and then he was ordained into the Church. He had studied theology and had passed his examinations with First Class Honours.

Soon after his ordination and he had started work in his Parish in Northumberland, the Bishop had asked him to return to Oxford.

He felt that this summons was somewhat unfair to the Parishioners on the estate, but it was too flattering an invitation to refuse.

Richard Brooke soon proved himself outstanding amongst the Parish Priests of the Oxford Diocese.

Ever since Tarena was a small child, her mother having died when she was only five, she had lived with her uncle.

She found him a wonderful substitute for the father she could not remember.

She had made many good friends in Oxford and the students spoilt her every time they came to the Vicarage to see her uncle.

At eighteen years old she was afraid that, if the Earl of Grandbrooke died, they would have to go and live in the North.

There had, of course, been an older uncle between the Earl and her Uncle Richard.

He was the Viscount, who was very handsome and much sought after. However, as a soldier he was sent to fight abroad and sadly lost his life in the Crimean War.

This had turned everything topsy-turvy.

It meant that, when the old Earl died and her Uncle Richard succeeded to the Earldom, he would undoubtedly have to abandon his career in the Church.

He would then have to look after the great ancestral home with its large estate in Northumberland that had been in the possession of the Grandbrookes for three centuries.

Tarena recognised that, as all her friends were in Oxford, she had no wish to go and live in the North.

She had indeed enjoyed visiting the ancestral home at Christmas, but last year the Earl had been in poor health and the party had not been as entertaining as it had been in previous years.

She could not envisage herself and her uncle being isolated there. They would be far too far away from all the interests they had in the South and would have to entertain considerably more than they did at present.

In point of fact, as she had learnt when she stayed at Grandbrooke Hall, any distinguished persons going to Northumberland expected to be invited by the Earl as a guest and parties had to be given for them.

Tarena thought even though she enjoyed them, it would be tedious to have to entertain continually.

When she looked back, she realised that most of the guests had been old. She was always the youngest and most often the only female present.

'I just could not bear to leave you,' she sighed to the flowers she had loved ever since she could remember.

Then, as she walked back to the house, she thought how cosy and comfortable they were in the Vicarage.

Her uncle had always been so kind to her and she realised how much he had adored his sister who was her mother.

Elizabeth had been the only daughter of the Earl.

She had often confessed that she had been spoilt by him and her brothers ever since she had been born.

It was a genuine tragedy to Tarena that she could not remember her mother very clearly.

She knew she had been soft, sweet and gentle and had cuddled her long after she was a baby and had sung her to sleep in a delightful soothing voice.

Tarena could hardly remember her father either.

He had been, she reckoned, very strong and tall and always carried her on his shoulders round the garden.

How and when he had died she could never quite find out and whenever she wanted to talk about him, her uncle changed the subject.

She found instead that they were talking about her mother and how pretty she had been when she was her age.

'Uncle Richard ought to be back by now,' Tarena mused.

She turned at the end of the garden to walk towards the house and then to her unbounded joy she saw him at the garden door.

With a little cry she ran towards him with her arms outstretched.

"You are back! You are back, Uncle Richard!" she exclaimed. "I have been so worried because I had not heard from you."

He kissed her most affectionately on both cheeks and then he suggested,

"Let's go into my study. I have a great deal to tell you."

Although his hair was turning a little grey and there were lines under his eyes, which had not been there a few years ago, he was still one of the best-looking men Tarena had ever seen – certainly the most handsome Cleric in the whole of Oxford.

They went into his comfortable study, which was filled with books that Tarena loved almost as much as she loved the garden.

She read avidly on every subject and her uncle was not so mean as to deprive her of the modern novels that were just becoming popular in the country.

In fact his library was an example, Tarena believed, to every other Clergyman to keep up with the times, as it would help them to understand what the younger members of their congregation were thinking and dreaming about.

"Have you had a difficult time, Uncle Richard?" Tarena asked, as he closed the door behind them.

"As I expect you may have guessed, my father has died," he replied. "I have to take his place as the Head of the family and the Master of Grandbrooke Hall."

Tarena sighed.

"Do we really have to leave Oxford and go North?" she asked him with a feeling of foreboding in her voice.

"I am afraid that I will have to," the new Earl of Grandbrooke answered her. "But there is something else I want to talk to you about."

Tarena looked at him in surprise.

He sat down in his favourite chair and she sat near him on one of the satin stools in front of the fireplace.

"First," her uncle began, "I must tell you that I am very glad I did not take you North with me. My father died soon after I arrived and it was not only very upsetting for all the staff, who had been with him for many years, but also for our many relations."

He sighed before he went on,

"They had no idea that he was so seriously ill, but they arrived, as you can imagine, almost every hour from every part of the country."

He spoke slowly and quietly.

Tarena knew that he had been extremely fond of his father and his death must have been a terrible shock.

In fact the old Earl had not yet reached the age of seventy and, although he had been in ill health for some time, no one had thought it was really serious.

Her uncle had stopped speaking and Tarena said in a small voice,

"So I suppose we will have to leave here where we have been so happy."

"I most certainly have to leave, but I want to talk to you, Tarena, about yourself and your father."

"My father?" Tarena exclaimed in astonishment. "But you have always told me so very little about him."

"What I have to tell you now is something that you were too young to understand in the past and I would not have told you even now if the Marquis of Salisbury had not been present at my father's funeral."

Tarena was listening to him wide-eyed.

She just could not understand why the Marquis of Salisbury, the then Secretary of State for Foreign Affairs, of whom she had often heard, had any connection in any way with her father.

Her uncle took a deep breath.

"Let's start at the beginning. Before you were born I came to Oxford to finish my education. It was a wise move on the part of my father, who thought I should enjoy Oxford and it would be an opportunity for me to excel, as he fervently hoped, at the University."

"So you enjoyed being a student?" asked Tarena.

"Very much. I became friends with a young man who was younger than me, but who happened to be in the same College and we shared a set of rooms. His name was Ivan and he came from the Balkans."

Tarena was listening to him intently and she did not interrupt.

"Ivan's surname was Sazon," her uncle continued. "Although a foreigner, he was soon accepted at Oxford for his athletic abilities. As he spoke excellent English, people soon forgot that he was of a different nationality."

Tarena wondered why her uncle was telling her all this, but she did not make any comment.

He went on,

"After I had received my degree and was ordained, I was asked to stay and help in the Cathedral. My father

6

thought it was an excellent idea. He was well aware that, once I took over a Parish Church on the estate, I would have very little time for anything else. 'Enjoy yourself, my boy,' he used to say when I first went up to Oxford. 'If you don't play cricket well or row in the Boat Race, I will be most annoyed with you'!"

He gave a little laugh.

"Ivan and I were almost partners. He was very good at cricket, became Captain of the College team and then played for the University."

"And you did too, Uncle Richard?"

"I could not let Ivan beat me and I was exceedingly proud that we both managed to be in the University cricket team and we beat Cambridge by five wickets!"

Tarena had heard all this before and she noticed a little elation in her uncle's voice.

"Then, when I was ordained, I was offered a small house to live in."

Tarena knew all this too, but she did not say so.

"Because I had a house, your mother, who was then eighteen and finding it rather boring in Northumberland, came to live with me. She was, of course, a huge success with all the undergraduates because she was so beautiful and so talented. She sang at their Concerts and danced better than any girl they had ever met."

He paused for a moment as if he was looking back into the past.

"Naturally, as Ivan was my very best friend, he was regularly a guest in my house, and not unnaturally he fell deeply in love with my sister, Elizabeth, and she fell head over heels in love with him."

He sighed before he added in a moving way,

"I have never known two people to be so incredibly happy together."

"So then you married them," Tarena came in as if she was anticipating the end of the story.

"Yes, I married them and although Ivan was too old to be a student, he managed to stay on by offering to coach the cricket team."

"But they lived with you – "

"As I was out and about so much, I did not interfere with them. Your mother, young though she was, ran the house brilliantly with the help of only two servants and we entertained a great deal. At the same time I realised that they were happiest when they could be alone together."

He was now speaking very slowly.

Tarena felt that he was looking back into the past and seeing it all happening again in his mind.

Equally she was becoming anxious for him to tell her something she did not already know, as he had always been so evasive when she had asked him more penetrating questions.

"It was after they had been married for nearly two years," her uncle went on, "that you were born. I have never seen two people more thrilled with their baby."

"I am glad they liked me," Tarena remarked softly.

"They really adored you, Tarena. You were such a beautiful baby that Ivan always said that you were an angel come down from Heaven and he was especially blessed by having you."

"Do tell me more," she begged. "I have never been able to discover very much about my father."

"That is just what I am about to do, Tarena, but it's not that easy."

Tarena stopped herself from asking him why.

8

After a moment or two he continued,

"You were only four years of age when what was a sublime dream of happiness between two delightful young people became a disaster."

"Disaster? What happened, Uncle Richard?"

"I had learnt secretly and he begged me not to tell anyone, that Ivan was in fact not just Ivan Sazon, as he had told everyone, but His Royal Highness the Prince Ivan of Karlova in the Balkans."

"His Royal Highness! You mean his father was a King!" exclaimed Tarena.

"Exactly. But his father was comparatively young and was therefore expected to reign for many more years. It was only when the Prime Minister of Karlova contacted Ivan did he realise that the situation was far more serious."

"What happened? *Do* tell me."

"We had known for some time that the Russians were trying to infiltrate into the Balkans and were moving forward steadily into Asia, in the process adding thousands of square miles to their already huge Empire."

He paused to see if Tarena was following him.

"Here in England Queen Victoria had appreciated the political situation far better than anyone else. She had then with the greatest difficulty persuaded Mr. Gladstone's Government, as it was in those days, that everything must be done to keep the Russians out of the Mediterranean."

"So what did my father do about it?" Tarena asked in a small voice.

"The officials who came to tell him that his father had died so unexpectedly, informed him of the impending danger from Russia. They were already infiltrating not just into Karlova, but also into Dubnik, another small country on their borders – it is in fact nearer to the Aegean Sea than Karlova."

"I really – don't understand," Tarena admitted.

"What they were really asking was that Ivan should go back to Karlova as King to save his own country, as well as the one adjacent to it, by marrying Princess Catrina of Dubnik. After her father's death, she had been left the Ruler of that country."

"But how could he – "

Her uncle held up his hand.

"Let me tell it my way, Tarena. As it is difficult to understand. What I actually knew and no one else was aware of, was that Ivan's marriage to my sister had never been announced. Ivan was anxious not to appear Royal in any way and thus be treated differently from his friends at Oxford.

"He had been so secretive about it that even his Ambassador in London had no idea that he was not single and therefore not free to marry Princess Catrina as they now wished."

He lowered his voice before he continued,

"They were very afraid that he would refuse and so they made it abundantly clear that, unless he did as they asked, the Russians would undoubtedly take over Dubnik, and then Karlova, without any difficulty and the people of the two countries could do nothing because they had no strong leader."

"I can understand that – part," she whispered, "but what – did he do?"

"When the officials left us, and, of course, they did not meet your mother, we talked for a long time. But Ivan knew where his duty lay. There was no one else to take his place and no one but him to save his people – and they were *his* people – unless he returned to Karlova and did as his Prime Minister asked of him."

"You mean he married the Princess – while he was still married to Mama?" Tarena asked in a horrified voice.

"There was nothing else he could do. Naturally it broke his heart and your mother's that they must part. But they had enjoyed six years of such perfect and wonderful happiness, which is much more than many people are able to claim in their whole lives."

"I can hardly believe it," murmured Tarena.

"That is just what I felt when it happened, but Ivan either had to sacrifice his own and Elizabeth's happiness or allow the two independent countries to pass into the hands of the Russians. That would have been disastrous not only for them but for the rest of the Balkans."

"So – he went away."

"It was agony for your mother and for him, but he swore that as soon as it was possible he would return or else ask her to join him. He did not know how it could be arranged, but he swore that he could not live without her."

There was a poignant silence, before Tarena added in a whisper,

"And then Mama died."

"She died not only because her heart was broken, but she did catch a very nasty cold that winter and did not take as much care of herself as she should have done."

"I think perhaps she was too unhappy – "

Her uncle nodded.

"I have often thought that myself. Perhaps people do really die of a broken heart and your mother without your father was indeed a very different woman from my sister, who had been so happy and who had made everyone around her happy too."

"So Mama died and what happened to my father?"

"He most certainly saved his own country as well as Dubnik by marrying the Princess Catrina. The Russians were not strong enough at that particular time to face the combined countries ready to fight them under their new leader, King Ivan, for their freedom and independence."

"So he really did save Karlova?"

"He most surely did and Princess Catrina's country as well."

"But he acted a lie in marrying her when he was already married to my mother," asserted Tarena.

"No one was aware of it except myself. When Ivan Sazon disappeared from Oxford, there was soon someone else to take his place on the cricket field. People had no idea that he was now King Ivan of Karlova and that he was admired and respected in another part of the world."

"And no one cared?" Tarena asked him.

"To be honest with you Ivan Sazon was very soon forgotten as younger men arrived. Of course, the students who took their degrees in his time left Oxford and a new generation peopled the cloisters."

"But *I* was still here," Tarena countered almost aggressively.

"Of course you were. I managed to convince any of our relatives who were at all curious, that your mother was now a widow. Her husband had died unexpectedly and had been buried without there being an official family funeral for them to attend."

"It must have been so very difficult for you, Uncle Richard – to lie as you had to."

"I have prayed to God to forgive me. At the same time I knew that it was the right thing for Ivan to do to be loyal to his own people and not to sacrifice them for his own happiness."

"So poor Mama – died too," Tarena replied with a sob. "I am very glad that I could stay with you."

"And I have loved having you, Tarena, and I have deliberately not arranged for you to meet too many of my family, because I did not wish you to feel embarrassed or to be asked questions you did not know the answers to."

"I am trying – to understand, but you can imagine, Uncle Richard, this is all – rather a shock to me."

"I am afraid that you will be even more shocked by what I have to suggest now – "

"What – can that be?" Tarena asked him nervously.

"At my father's funeral, as I have already told you, one of those attending was the Marquis of Salisbury, the Secretary of State for Foreign Affairs. He informed me that my friend, Ivan, your father, had a dreadful accident some years ago when out riding. Although he continued to rule, he has been a sick man for the last two years."

"Really – ill?"

"He died a month ago. As he and Princess Catrina had no children, a distant relative of hers has now offered himself to succeed Ivan."

"And you think he will be able to keep the Russians away?" Tarena enquired.

"It is the right question to ask. The Marquis has assured me it is only possible if, as has happened in so many other of the Balkan States, Queen Victoria gives him the protection of Britain by providing him with a British wife."

"I do know that, as I have been reading about it in the newspapers."

"The Marquis also told me that a Headquarters has been set up in the Russian Legation at Bucharest, presided over by a man called Hitrovo. He is a formidable operator who has made trouble for Prince Alexander of Battenberg."

"I do remember the story about Prince Alexander!" Tarena exclaimed.

"Now, and this is a secret, the Department of the Russian Foreign Office that deals with all Balkan countries has provided Hitrovo with three million roubles to pursue his campaign."

He paused as if to see that his niece was listening and then continued,

"His task is to find dissident Bulgarians who will organise a revolution to thrust Bulgaria into the Russian orbit."

"Has anyone tried to stop him?"

"They have a formidable opponent in a man called Stambulov, the thirty-two year old Co-Regent of Bulgaria. The Marquis met him and said he knows every weapon in the Russian Armoury. Even so the situation is extremely dangerous. The Queen herself is very worried as to what will happen unless the Bulgarians themselves are greatly strengthened by their Rulers.

"There have been a number of warning incidents that have scared the weak-hearted in Bulgaria and made it absolutely clear to the Queen that whatever happens we must not allow Russia to take over the whole of that part of the world as they so obviously wish to do."

"No! No! Of course not," Tarena cried.

"The Marquis also informed me that London is at the moment swept by a new wave of anti-Russian feeling. The Russians have indeed failed dismally in their attempt to capture Constantinople. The Marquis told me secretly that General Gorchakov had said to Mr. Disraeli, 'we have sacrificed a hundred thousand men and a hundred million roubles for an illusion'."

"How ghastly," Tarena murmured.

"He apparently said this, but the Marquis told me the Russian standing in the Balkans is stronger than it has ever been before. We must somehow prevent them going any further without actually resorting to war."

"That seems extremely difficult, when it is all so far away. If they are infiltrating into Bulgaria, how are we in England to stop them? We will not know about it until they are actually there."

"That is a very sensible remark, Tarena. That is why, my dearest, we have to support the Bulgarians. Not by fighting with guns, but by a more subtle means. One thing we are quite convinced of is that the Russians dare not face open war with England. At the same time they are determined to take over what countries they can before it is too late for us to stop them."

"So what can we do, Uncle Richard?"

"It is to have the Union Jack flying high wherever possible. That is why I am going to ask a great sacrifice of you, but it would save Karlova and Dubnik from being lost to the Russians."

Tarena's eyes seemed to open until they filled her whole face.

"Me! I don't – understand what you are saying."

"I have told the Marquis that you are in fact not only the niece of the Earl of Grandbrooke but also *Princess Tarena of Karlova.*"

Tarena stared at him.

Once again she mumbled in a voice that did not sound like her own,

"I don't know – what you are saying – or what you are suggesting, Uncle Richard."

"What the Marquis is suggesting, and I believe that it will save Karlova, is that you marry Prince Igor, who is taking over after your father's death, with the blessing of

Queen Victoria and the protection of the Union Jack. And the Russians would then not dare to interfere or infiltrate into either Karlova or Dubnik."

"But how can I – do it? How will the people accept me when they know that their King – who ruled them for so long was still married – to my mother at the same time as – he was married to Princess Catrina?"

She stumbled over the words as if it was virtually impossible for her to say them.

There was a sympathetic expression in her uncle's eyes as he gazed at her.

"Let me make it very clear," he said, "that no one knew that your father was still married when he married Princess Catrina. What I have assured the Marquis and what he fully believes, is that your mother died the year after you were born and so your father was therefore a widower when he married again."

"*But that is a lie!*"

"I realise that and I am very ashamed of myself for having to lie. But it is a lie to save the lives of thousands of people from the Russian menace. I do feel that, if your mother was still alive, she would be willing to tell such a small lie for the sake of the country that the man she loved so much belonged to."

"I suppose two years one way or another – does not matter much," Tarena agreed. "Equally must I really go – to Karlova to marry a man whom I have never even seen – and who will certainly not want to marry me?"

"He has already, through the Prime Minister and the Ambassador of Karlova, asked Queen Victoria to send him a bride. Her Majesty was, the Marquis has told me, in despair because there was no one suitable available. She has already provided many English brides for her relations on the Continent."

He paused for a moment before he carried on,

"The Marquis was absolutely certain that the Queen would be delighted if you would do as they ask and take, in your own person, a weapon to Karlova, which will frighten away the Russians more effectively than any gun or Army of trained soldiers."

Tarena was silenced.

She could hardly believe that this was not part of a dream and she felt that she would soon wake up and find it was all untrue.

Never could she have imagined that anything like this would be asked of her.

Because she had always been told how happy her father and mother were together, she had hoped that one day she herself would fall in love.

A wonderful man would love her just for herself and they would live happily ever after.

Was it possible that her kind and loving uncle was asking her to travel to an unknown far-off country that was in danger?

She would then save it, as apparently her father had done by deserting her mother and marrying some woman he had never even seen.

'How can I do it?' she asked herself desperately. 'How *can* I?'

She became aware that her uncle was watching her with an expression on his face she had never seen before.

"How can I, Uncle Richard?" she asked aloud.

"I have been thinking it over all the way back from the North, Tarena, I believe it is God's will that you should help these people and save them."

'No! No!' Tarena tried to scream, but the words would not come.

"Your father gave up everything he cared for," he continued, "because he knew that without him his country would be lost. Now you have to follow his lead because his blood is yours and save his country once again."

"Suppose – I refuse?" she whispered.

Her uncle made a wide gesture with his hands.

"No one will force you to do anything you feel you cannot do and against your will, my dearest."

"But I want to stay here with you, Uncle Richard. I want to find someone who loves me and marry a man with whom I will be as happy as you say Mama was with Papa."

There was silence for a moment and then he asked,

"Could you be really happy, Tarena, knowing that you are condemning your father's country to which you, as his child, belong as well, to a life that for many of them would be worse than death?"

There was complete silence.

Her uncle was praying that she would understand the urgency of his request.

Tarena rose from her chair and walked over to the window.

She stood looking out over the garden she loved so much that had been planned by her mother.

She reflected as to how happy she had been without parents throughout these many years she had spent with her uncle.

This was her home.

This was where she had thought she would belong until she made a home of her own.

Then she closed her eyes, as if the sun was blinding her, and prayed fervently for guidance in a way she had never prayed before.

'*Help me God*! Please tell me what I am to do.' she prayed. 'How can I do this when I am not even trained for it? Tell me the answer.'

Then, just as she opened her eyes, a bright shaft of sunlight blazed through the window.

Suddenly she felt as if someone touched her face very gently, as if she heard a voice that she knew, although she could not remember it – it had to be her father's.

She could hear it quite clearly in her mind.

'You must save my people, Tarena. They are now yours and you cannot allow them to suffer."

She turned round to see her uncle gazing lovingly at her.

"Very – well, Uncle Richard," she said hesitantly, "I will try to do – as you ask. But I am terribly frightened. Unless you help me and – unless I am told exactly what to do, I would rather die than make a mess of it."

He smiled and held out his hands.

"I knew you would understand. You are not your father's daughter for nothing. Although it was an agony beyond words for Ivan to leave your mother, he did what he felt God wanted him to do and he was a great success."

"Do you think that I can be too?" Tarena asked.

"As Ivan's daughter you will be received with open arms. Don't forget that he belonged to them and was a part of them. When you take his place, they will love you as they loved him."

"How could he have left Mama when they were so happy?"

There was a pause before Uncle Richard replied,

"The night before he left I had a long talk with Ivan. He said to me, 'it is an agony beyond words for me to leave everything I love and everything that matters to me, but I believe, as I know you believe, Richard, it is a call from God'."

There was silence and then Tarena sighed,

"I only hope if God helped Papa to save Karlova, which you say he did, then He will help me as well."

"The answer to that, Tarena, is that I will pray for you every day and you must pray for yourself. It is what you learnt to do when you were a child and I promise you that God and your Guardian Angel will never desert you."

"I suppose that should be very reassuring, but I am really frightened, Uncle Richard, that, when I do reach Karlova, suppose Prince Igor does not like me?"

He smiled.

"You are very beautiful, my dearest, and you are English. Like your father, he is desperate to keep Karlova and Dubnik free from the Russians. The most important factor, as you are aware, is the people themselves and he is handicapped because he comes from Dubnik."

"What you are saying, Uncle Richard, is that they will believe because of Papa that I am part of them."

"Exactly. In fact they will recognise you now as their rightful Queen. But if you reigned alone, you could find it very difficult to withstand the Russians. If, on the other hand, you marry this Prince Igor, you could together rescue both countries through the strength of your union."

"Then I can only pray that the situation will be better than it seems at present."

Tarena thought for a moment and then asked,

"I expect you are giving up this house and your Parish anyway, Uncle Richard?"

"I have to, although it's a home I love and have no wish to leave," the new Earl replied.

"That makes two of us. So I suppose we can only hope that in our new lives we will find the same happiness we have enjoyed up to now."

Quite suddenly she gave a little cry,

"I cannot bear it, Uncle Richard. It's too much to ask. How can I possibly go away from everything I know and everything I love?"

She threw herself against him and he put his arms around her.

"I know exactly what you are feeling, my dearest, and I will want to cry myself when I leave Oxford which has meant so much to me. But we are both called to a new life and we have to make the very best of it.

"Where you are concerned, my dear, you have to make sure that the people of Karlova love you as much as they all loved your father – and that should not be too difficult."

"It seems impossible to me and there will be no one there who knows me or cares for me!"

"I think you will be surprised to find how many people will be looking forward to seeing you and will be thrilled and grateful because you are coming to save them."

Tarena was crying too much to answer.

There was an expression of pain in her uncle's eyes as he held her close.

Then he was praying – praying silently to God who had never failed him yet, that she would be happy as well as successful.

And that the new challenge in her life would not be as difficult as she feared it would be.

CHAPTER TWO

Early the next morning they set off for London.

They had stayed up late talking about the situation and Tarena had learnt from her uncle a great deal more about her father than she had been told before.

By the time she retired, she was finally convinced that the only course she could take was to follow in her father's footsteps and help his people who were now hers.

When she was in bed, she thought of Prince Igor with a little shudder.

Then she told herself she must be fair and not make any decisions about him until they actually met.

"What we have to do," her Uncle Richard had said to her, "is to buy you a complete trousseau. You cannot go to Karlova to be Queen in the clothes you are wearing now. We will have to shop quickly and naturally expensively. Luckily I can now well afford it."

To his relief Tarena gave a little laugh.

"That is some consolation at any rate," she smiled. "I must have a really fantastic wedding gown."

"Of course, of course," he agreed hurriedly.

Fortunately he had driven down from the North in a chaise drawn by a team of extremely fine horses that had belonged to his father.

And now they set off at a pace that Tarena felt she had never travelled at before.

She was fascinated to find how well her uncle could drive them and when she told him so, he replied,

"Actually, I always drove my father's best horses even when I was young. I have indeed missed, but I have not said so, a team like this since I have been a Parson."

They reached London in what Tarena was certain was a record time and went straight to Grandbrooke House in Belgrave Square.

It had been closed up for the last five years since the late Earl had been so ill and only two old servants had been kept on there as caretakers.

They were delighted to see the new Earl and Tarena when they arrived.

"It's been real lonely here, my Lord," the butler said. "No one came from the North to see us. Although several relatives popped in when they was in London, we sometimes went months without seeing any of the family."

"Well, I am afraid that we will not be with you for long, Simpkins," the Earl replied. "But I intend to come to London at least once or twice a month and so you must engage any extra servants you need to keep the house in good order."

Tarena could see that the butler was delighted at this piece of news.

As they had arrived late and without warning, a somewhat scanty luncheon was provided for them.

However, Simpkins promised that the cook, who was his wife, would serve them a delicious dinner.

Tarena would have really liked to explore the house as she had never seen it before, but her uncle insisted that they should go at once to Bond Street.

"I promised the Marquis of Salisbury that we would leave as soon as possible," he explained. "I have an idea that Her Majesty might wish to see you tomorrow, so we must shop while we have the chance."

"The Queen!" exclaimed Tarena. "Do you really think that she will want to see me?"

"I am sure she will. She is very worried about the Russians and is determined to circumvent their ambitions as far as she can."

Bond Street was a delight that Tarena had never experienced before.

Her uncle with his keen eye for detail had taken the trouble, after speaking to the Marquis, to find out from his relatives and others in the know who came to his father's funeral which were the best shops.

"We have to make quick decisions," he told Tarena. "Therefore just calculate what you will require to impress your new countrymen who have not, I would suppose, seen very much of current French fashions."

"What about Princess Catrina?" Tarena asked.

Her uncle smiled.

"I was told most confidentially that she is not very prepossessing and had no dress sense or made herself as spectacular as a Queen should be."

Tarena sighed.

"Poor Papa, he must have hated having someone who was not beautiful as Mama – as his wife."

"I think he must have suffered, as perhaps no other man has suffered in all those long years when he knew they would never meet again."

"I think now they are together," Tarena said softly, "and Mama will be happy again."

The Earl did not say anything.

But he thought that it was very touching that his niece should be so sure that her father and mother were now as one.

And he did everything in his power to make her feel more confident in herself.

When, as he expected, a call came from Windsor Castle, they drove off together the following morning.

As soon as the carriage wheels started, he said,

"You look very lovely, my dear, and in my opinion exactly as a young Queen should be."

Tarena laughed.

"I would never have thought of myself as a Queen, but I am sure that I will make a thousand mistakes and then people will laugh at me."

"I think that is most unlikely," he replied. "I have always found that you are never at a loss to say the right words and do the right thing."

He smiled before he continued,

"People in Oxford used to tell me how much they admired the way you looked after my guests for me and played the part of hostess at the Vicarage when you were still only twelve or thirteen."

"The Vicarage is one thing, but a Palace and a large country are quite another. I am just wondering how I can possibly get to know the Karlovans."

"I am sure you will find it will all come to you when you arrive and I am certain that your father will be helping you in every way he possibly can."

Tarena smiled at him wistfully.

"It seems rather strange, but I am sure of that too. Although I am frightened and want to stay in England with you, I can feel Papa pulling me towards Karlova!"

When they arrived at Windsor Castle, Tarena was overawed by the immensity of it all, also the number of equerries and Statesmen who were waiting to meet her.

The Marquis of Salisbury introduced her to them and the Earl became aware that they were delighted by her beauty and the manner in which she conducted herself.

She might be scared, but she did not show it.

When they were both finally ushered into Queen Victoria's private sitting room, Tarena's curtsy was exactly as it should be.

"I am very delighted, Princess Tarena," the Queen began, "that you are going to Karlova and you will, I am sure, save it from being taken over by the Russians. And I feel certain you understand that no time must be lost in filling the empty throne."

"I do understand, Your Majesty," Tarena replied.

"We know very little about Prince Igor of Dubnik," the Queen went on, "who has, I understand, been holding the fort ever since your father died and, the sooner you are on the throne, the more difficult it will be for the Russians to infiltrate into the country."

There was nothing Tarena could say except that she was very grateful to receive Her Majesty's blessing.

"Now that I have seen you," the Queen declared, "I think that you are exactly what Karlova needs and, as your father was so popular, there is no doubt that you will be equally welcome."

"I will do my best, Your Majesty. And I can only pray that I will receive every possible help from those who are already there."

"To make sure of that," the Queen stated, "I have instructed the Marquis of Salisbury to have you taken to the Kingdom of Karlova in one of our newest and most impressive Ironclads."

Tarena's eyes sparkled.

"I have always wanted to travel on one of the large Battleships and it will be a most spectacular way to arrive. Oh, I thank Your Majesty, thank you, thank you."

The Queen smiled at her enthusiasm.

When she left, she told the Earl, who had stayed behind, that she was very taken by his niece.

"She is exactly the sort of girl we want to put on the small thrones," she stipulated, "and make sure the wicked Russians do not, as they are constantly trying to do, work up the people against their Rulers."

"I feel sure that Your Majesty is right," the Earl said, "and my niece will undoubtedly capture their hearts."

The Queen gave a little sigh.

"I wish we knew more about this Prince Igor," she said, "but apparently he has had very little contact with our Ambassador in Karlova and has spent nearly all his time in Dubnik, his own country."

"I am sure when he sees my niece, Your Majesty, he will fall in love with her," added the Earl.

He was thinking of how much Tarena resembled her mother and that Ivan had lost his heart the moment he saw her.

"As you are going to Karlova with your niece," Queen Victoria was saying. "I feel sure you will be able to give me a clear and unbiased report on the Prime Minister and the Cabinet at Karlova."

"Of course, I will be honoured to do whatever Your Majesty requires."

"I am always afraid when a King, who was as much loved at King Ivan was, dies," the Queen said reflectively, "that they find it hard to start again at the beginning with someone new. That can lead to a dangerous situation of which the Russians will undoubtedly take advantage."

"I will report all that I find to Your Majesty as soon as I return, but if things are very difficult, Your Majesty will understand that it might be wise for me to stay and support Tarena until we are quite sure that both she and the throne are safe."

"Of course, of course," the Queen agreed. "But I will look forward to seeing you again and I am happy that you will be able to spare time from your magnificent house in Northumberland to be here with me at Windsor."

"Your Majesty is very gracious," the Earl replied.

He bowed his way from the sitting room to join Tarena, who was wondering why he was taking so long.

"Did Her Majesty disapprove of me?" she asked him, a bit nervously.

"On the contrary, my dearest, she was so delighted with you and feels sure that you will save Karlova from the enemy as your father managed to do for so many years."

"I only wish that my father was here now," Tarena murmured beneath her breath.

The Earl knew she was thinking of the man she had to marry and was apprehensive as to what he might be like.

He then talked to the Ambassador and various other officials who had come from Karlova.

They were vague about Prince Igor and apparently knew very little about him.

He was over thirty and had, as far as the Earl could ascertain, seldom left his house, which was on the far side of Dubnik, to visit the Palace in Karlova.

"You are quite certain that he is the only candidate for the throne?" the Earl asked the Karlovan Ambassador privately. "Surely there must be other young Princes we can turn to if my niece finds Prince Igor unacceptably unattractive."

"If there are, then I know nothing about them," the Ambassador replied. "When the late King Ivan was in good health, he gave quite a number of parties at the Palace which we all enjoyed. But now I think about it, there were no young men with any pretence of Royal blood."

*

There were two more days of shopping.

As they started early in the morning and did not end until nearly dinnertime, Tarena said she had enough clothes to last her for a hundred years.

Her uncle laughed.

"On the contrary, my dearest, I am prepared to bet that in six months or so you will be saying you have not a thing to wear and are preparing to travel to Paris!"

"I will do nothing of the sort," Tarena asserted. "I think buying clothes is an awful bore. But I have chosen two attractive riding habits that I am certain will convince the natives that I am more anxious to please the horses than anyone else!"

He laughed again.

"Now you must not say things like that or they will undoubtedly take offence. Tell me about your wedding dress."

"It is absolutely fantastic. It had really been a show gown to attract people into the shop and was not actually for sale. They were reluctant to let me have it. But I knew it would look very glamorous in the Cathedral – if indeed there is one in Karlova."

"Of course there is one. And I intend to marry you with everything possible to make it the most memorable day of your life."

"I will be thinking how glad I am that it is you, Uncle Richard, who is marrying me and not some strange Priest I have never seen before."

"He will doubtless be an Archbishop, who will think I am being very pushy in joining you to your husband when it should really be his job."

"It is quite easy," Tarena exclaimed. "Tell him, if I don't have you to marry me, I will not be married at all!"

The Earl held up his hands.

"Now that is just the sort of comment you must never make. Remember, Tarena, Queens are always very dignified and give an impression of extreme grandeur."

Tarena made a face.

"You know I will never be like that. I just want to be myself. If I have to sit all day on a golden throne while people curtsy in front of me, I shall run away and come back to you in England!"

He knew that she was just teasing.

However, he was feeling somewhat worried that she would find it boring being Queen to some strange man she did not love.

There could be the extreme loneliness her mother had felt when her beloved Ivan had left her.

'There must be some young people in Karlova with whom she can laugh and play as she should do at her age,' he thought to himself. 'She should not be forced to take on the heavy and often exceedingly dreary affairs of State.'

There was nothing he could do but pray.

He hoped to find some sympathetic Karlovans who would understand Tarena's difficulties before he had to leave her and return to England.

*

At the moment, however, they were being heavily pressed by the Ambassador to leave as quickly as possible.

He was so agitated that the Earl was convinced that the situation was far worse that he had told Her Majesty.

When he questioned the Ambassador, he confided,

"We have had a great deal of difficulty, as you may not know in England, over who should reign on the throne of Bulgaria."

"I did realise that there was some trouble," the Earl replied, "but I understood that you had found a suitable candidate."

The Ambassador gave a somewhat forced laugh.

"The Bulgarian Assembly," he said, "invited Prince Waldemar of Denmark, a brother of the Czarina of Russia and the Princess of Wales to take the Crown, but the Czar vetoed the suggestion."

"I did hear that."

"King Charles of Romania was approached, but he also retreated before Russia's scowls."

"What happened then?"

"Finally, we were all startled and astonished when twenty-seven year old Prince Ferdinand of Saxe-Coburg, a Cousin of Queen Victoria, accepted the throne."

"Now you are bringing it back to me. I understand he is a very strange man."

"Very strange indeed, my Lord," the Ambassador replied. "He wears bracelets and powders his face and sleeps in pink nightgowns trimmed with Valenciennes lace. His nerves are so finely strung that he consults only ladies' doctors."

"Good Heavens!" the Earl exclaimed. "I had no idea of all this."

"As no one else seems willing to run the risk of being assassinated by the wily Russians, Prince Stambulov accepted him because he is both rich and well-born."

The Earl threw up his hands and sighed,

"Money always turns the balance."

"That is true, my Lord. His mother doted on him and always believed that one day he would wear a crown and therefore, as you can well understand, he accepted the throne without demur."

"What did Queen Victoria say about it?"

"She was dismayed as she had always thought that Alexander of Battenburg might return."

"So King Ferdinand is now firmly established in Bulgaria?"

The Ambassador laughed.

"There is no doubt that the rough Bulgarians who appeared in Tirnovo to watch the Prince take the oath were astonished by his appearance. His hands and wrists were covered in many rings and bracelets. His long robe made of purple velvet and ermine was easily grand enough for an Emperor *and* his hair smelt of pomade."

The Earl laughed as if he could not help it.

He remembered now hearing that King Ferdinand had a small pointed beard, piercing blue eyes and a huge nose that soon became the delight of caricaturists.

So Bulgaria was now settled, but there was little doubt that, while Karlova was for the moment without a King, the Russians would attempt to take the country over.

The Earl kept his worries to himself.

But he found it difficult to sleep the night before they were to board the Battleship.

The Royal Sovereign was coming up the Thames to pick them up by the House of Commons.

When the Earl knelt to pray, he was wondering if in his anxiety to help 'Ivan's people,' he was now sending his beloved niece, Tarena, to a horrible death.

The next morning there was much amusement over the large amount of luggage Tarena was to take aboard the Battleship.

She travelled in a closed carriage with her uncle and the Ambassador and behind them came two large vans piled with trunks and hat-boxes.

The Battleship seemed larger and more imposing than Tarena had expected and when she first saw it, she whispered to her uncle,

"Now I really do feel grand. It's the most beautiful ship I have ever imagined."

"Her Majesty the Queen is really determined you will make an impressive arrival," the Ambassador told her.

"How could I do anything else on a ship I see is called *The Royal Sovereign*?"

The Earl was deeply impressed by the Battleship as well when they went aboard.

They met the Ambassador's wife, who was charged with chaperoning Tarena to Karlova and a Baroness who was to be her Lady-in-Waiting until she appointed her own after her arrival.

They curtsied to Tarena, which was something she had not anticipated.

Then a young man dressed very smartly in military uniform came forward and saluted the Ambassador.

"Oh, here you are, Count," called the Ambassador. "I am waiting to introduce you to the Princess."

He then moved across the cabin to where Tarena was talking animatedly to the Ambassador's wife.

"I would like, Your Royal Highness," he said, "to present to you Count Vladimir Sazon, who is in charge of the soldiers who are escorting you on the voyage."

Tarena turned round and saw that the newcomer was a tall very good-looking young man.

She held out her hand to him and he bowed over it respectfully.

And then she asked him,

"Did the Ambassador say that your name is Sazon? Then surely you must be of the same blood as my family?"

"It is something I am most honoured to be, Your Royal Highness," he responded. "I am a cousin, though distant, of His Majesty, your father, who I greatly admired and who was kind enough to give me my appointment of command of the Palace guard."

"Then you knew my father?" Tarena exclaimed. "As I expect you know, I have not seen him since I was only a child when he left England behind to become the King of Karlova."

"There is so much I can tell Your Royal Highness about His Majesty. He was loved by everyone in Karlova, as I am sure you yourself will be."

Tarena smiled at him.

"I can only hope your prophecy will come true."

"I was just thinking," said the Ambassador, "that as Count Sazon is a relation of Your Royal Highness, it is he who should teach you our language while we are travelling to Karlova. I daresay you will find it rather difficult, but it is important for you to speak to our people in their own tongue."

"I have thought of that already," Tarena answered. "I have read that the language of Karlova is a mixture of Greek and German and I already know Greek. Thus it will not be as difficult for me as it might be for someone else."

"I can be a hard taskmaster, Your Royal Highness," the Count smiled. "I know how important it is for you to understand what is being said and I myself have struggled away with many different languages since I was appointed to the Palace."

"Then you must help me to be fluent in Karlovan, Count Vladimir."

"As soon as the ship moves," the Count promised, "we will start talking to each other and to the others aboard in the language of Karlova. I have always thought it more attractive than other Balkan languages."

"Wonderful," Tarena exclaimed.

"I promise Your Royal Highness that, by the time we arrive, you will speak fluently so that everyone can understand you."

"Now I think you are boasting for both of you," the Earl came in. "At the same time I am delighted to know that my niece will have such a determined teacher."

They were seen off by the Marquis of Salisbury and a number of other Statesmen.

When he said goodbye to Tarena, he added,

"I want to thank you more than I can put into words for undertaking this task. I was almost in despair about what I could do for Karlova when I met your uncle at his father's funeral and learnt of your existence."

"As most people dislike funerals," Tarena replied, "I am sure you have been rewarded for being so kind as to attend my grandfather's."

"Actually our families have known each other for a long time," the Marquis smiled. "He spoilt me by letting me ride on his horses in steeplechases and point-to-points. When I won, it was entirely due to his generosity."

Tarena laughed.

"I do hope, my Lord, when my mission to Karlova is so important, that I don't disappoint you."

"I sincerely think you are going to be superb!"

The Marquis raised her hand to kiss it.

Then, as he turned to leave, he put his hand on the Count's shoulder.

"Please look after this beautiful Princess and don't let anyone hurt or upset her."

"You can trust me, my Lord," the Count replied. "And I am perfectly prepared to dedicate my life to anyone so beautiful."

The Marquis chuckled at this, but the Earl, who was listening, thought that it was a great advantage to have so pleasant a young man on the Battleship with them.

It might at least distract Tarena from her fears of what lay ahead.

Her first request was to explore the ship and the Count took her below to shake hands with the ten men who were her bodyguard.

She was introduced by the Captain of *The Royal Sovereign* to the members of his crew and they were all delighted to meet her.

She guessed that it was unusual for passengers on one of Her Majesty's Battleships to meet the entire crew.

Unusual too, as she had done, to invite the Captain and his Officers to dine with her.

The Captain was delighted at her invitation.

And when they sat down to dinner, joined by the Count and the other members of the party, it was a most jovial evening.

The Earl had been afraid that Tarena might have felt miserable at leaving England.

They were, however, all laughing as they steamed down the Thames.

By the time *The Royal Sovereign* had reached the English Channel, Tarena was beginning to feel rather more relaxed and that she was starting a new exciting adventure.

*

When she woke the next morning and found a note under her door, she realised how efficient the Count was.

In flowery language, which she felt he wrote with a twinkle in his eye, he informed her that lessons began at nine-thirty precisely.

Pupils are asked not to be late unless they are overcome by seasickness!

The sea, as they sailed down the English Channel, was quite calm.

When Tarena joined the Count on deck, the sun was shining and the huge Battleship, she thought, seemed to be moving swiftly and smoothly towards an El Dorado.

Tarena had put on one of the simple but very pretty dresses she had thought would be appropriate to wear on board ship.

Because she had thought it unnecessary, there was nothing covering her long auburn hair which caught the sunshine as she walked towards the Count.

He had arranged two chairs and a small table in a corner of the deck and, as she sat down, Tarena enquired,

"Do I also have to write?"

"Of course. I have already put down a list of verbs for you to memorise and as your teacher I would naturally expect you to be word perfect tomorrow morning!"

"I thought I was going to be able to enjoy a rest on board this ship," Tarena countered teasingly. "But I now foresee it's going to be hard work until we reach Port."

"It will not be as bad as that," the Count replied, "and I have a feeling that Your Royal Highness is going to be very quick at picking up the language that as you rightly said is a mixture of other languages of which you already have quite a knowledge."

"I know enough to be able to read books in Greek and most other European languages. I hope because my father was, I understand, a brilliant linguist, that I will be the same."

"Of course you will and your father was, without exception, the cleverest and most interesting man I have ever met."

"Do tell me more about him – "

He answered her without warning in her father's language and to her joy she found she could understand most of what he said.

When she stopped him and made him explain to her again in Greek or German what he had said, she knew it was a lesson she would not easily forget.

Tarena enjoyed the Count's tuition so much that it went on until luncheon time.

When the Earl came to tell them that luncheon was ready, he asked the Count how they had progressed.

"I can see that in a day or so I will no longer be required as a teacher," the Count replied. "I only hope I will not be confined to Barracks and forgotten until we step ashore!"

"Of course that will not happen! cried Tarena. "I have a great deal to ask you about Karlova, which will take you the whole voyage to answer."

"I am only too willing to oblige," said the Count. "But now I admit to feeling hungry and naturally thirsty."

They were laughing as they walked to the Captain's cabin and, as Tarena was such an important passenger, he had made way for her.

It was a very large room with, in one corner, as was traditional, a four-poster bed and on the other side there was sufficient space to entertain a large number of people.

They would eat at the long table or recline on a wide sofa or sit in comfortable armchairs.

In contrast, as the Captain told Tarena, the rest of the ship was overcrowded.

As well as Tarena's entourage, there was the crew and the bodyguard.

The midshipmen were having to sleep on the floor in one of the cabins and, as they were young boys, when they stopped at Gibraltar, Tarena insisted on buying large boxes of sweetmeats for them as well as more sophisticated presents for the Captain and his Officers.

"You will spoil them for other visitors who are not so generous," the Count suggested. "Equally I can assure you that they are worshipping at Your Royal Highness's feet which is undoubtedly what everyone else in Karlova will do when we arrive."

"You must write me a speech which I can make at a suitable opportunity," Tarena said, "saying how pleased I am to be where my father has been before me and hoping they will love me as much as they loved him."

"I think you can say that without my writing it for you. If people really think I have taught you to speak the language in such a short time, I will be tempted to give up the Army to take on pupils and charge them a huge fee for teaching them!"

Tarena laughed.

"I am sure you enjoy the Army far too much!"

"What I think we should do when we move out of here," said the Count, looking round at Gibraltar, "is to have some exercise. I have bought a deck tennis set that has just been invented for use on board ship. I am certain you would excel at it, Your Royal Highness."

As Tarena played extremely good lawn tennis, she found she could make the Count work very hard to be able to beat her at deck tennis.

In fact when she did beat him, she clapped her hands with delight.

"It's the first time, I assure you," he sighed, "I have ever been beaten by a woman. It's a failure that will not occur again!"

"Well, I am determined it will," Tarena boasted. "Therefore we will both have to exert ourselves."

The sea had been rough in the Bay of Biscay as they sailed through, but Tarena had not been upset.

However, the Ambassador's wife and the Baroness retired to their cabins and were not seen again until they reached Gibraltar.

"Everything will be much smoother from now on," the Count promised. "So I suppose you will have to spend some of your time with the ladies and I will not be able to have as much of you as I have had recently."

"I have no intention of talking, except, of course, politely in the morning and evening to the Ambassador's wife and the Baroness. I want to take more and more exercise and, if we cannot play deck tennis, then I will race you round the deck."

"I think that would be rather undignified. Much as I would love to see you running, I think it would be better if we exercised ourselves by dancing."

Tarena's eyes lit up.

"What a wonderful idea!" she exclaimed excitedly. "But what music is there to dance to?"

"I have discovered that two of my men earn money, when they are not on duty, by playing for people to dance in the village they come from."

"What do they play?" Tarena asked.

"One of them plays the piano and, if there is not one on board, which I think there is, he has a guitar and the other has a violin."

Tarena clapped her hands together.

"That is marvellous! Oh, do let's dance. I am sure my uncle will think it an excellent idea too. I believe he was a great dancer when he was a young man."

"Then he can dance with the Baroness," the Count suggested. "I have every intention of dancing with Your Royal Highness."

"And I want to dance with you – "

Their eyes met and for the briefest moment it was difficult to look away.

Then Tarena said quickly,

"The sun is still shining and I think we should play deck tennis."

They went out into the fresh air.

Tarena was thinking that it would be a mistake if she grew too fond of Count Vladimir, as it would make her all the more hostile to the man she had to marry when she arrived at Karlova.

She had not talked to anyone about Prince Igor and she gathered that her uncle knew very little about him.

'Surely they should tell me,' she thought, 'how old he is and what are his interests.'

She had the frightening feeling that because they were so afraid of the Russians, they would arrange for the wedding to take place almost before she had even met the Prince or had a chance to get to know him.

Then she thought that they could not force her to do anything she really detested.

'After all I will be Queen,' she said to herself, 'and they must listen to what I have to say and obey at least some of my commands.'

However she dare not say this even to her uncle.

When she thought about Prince Igor, she felt that there was something mysterious, even sinister, about him.

That was why she was told so little about him.

Even the Count seemed to avoid any conversation with her about him.

*

The Royal Sovereign moved steadily and sedately down the Mediterranean.

Tarena was sure she was going to find something unpleasant that for the moment was deliberately being kept from her.

'I must know more about him before I marry him,' she pondered again and again.

Finally she could not bear it any longer and so she asked to see her uncle.

"Why does no one talk to me about Prince Igor?" she demanded. "Surely I should know something about this man before I actually marry him."

Her uncle smiled.

"I think the truth is, my dearest, they know nothing about him themselves. As far as I can determine your father did not meet Prince Igor. He kept himself to himself and lived on the far side of Dubnik over four days journey from the Palace at Karlova."

"Well, if we are married, he can hardly live in one Palace and me in another."

"Of course not," the Earl said quickly. "But you must forgive me for not knowing anything about the man except that he is the only person of any real importance in Dubnik. He therefore must take a significant part in the governing of the Kingdom in the future."

That sounded reasonable.

Equally Tarena was gradually being convinced that there was something strange about Prince Igor they had not told her.

When she thought about it at night, she felt herself shiver.

It did seem most strange that no one had anything particularly good to say about him, even though they did not say anything unpleasant.

They rounded the South of Greece and steamed up the Aegean.

Tarena found her uncle sitting alone on deck when she had just finished another game of deck tennis with the Count. She sat down and slipped her arm through his.

"What are you thinking about, Uncle Richard?" she enquired.

"I was thinking about you, my dear," he answered.

"And I have been thinking about myself. I want you to promise me that I will not be pushed into marrying Prince Igor until we have met each other several times and talked privately together."

"Of course that is my idea too, but I must be honest and tell you, my dearest, that the Ambassador thinks the Prime Minister and everyone in the Cabinet will want your marriage to be solemnised as quickly as possible after you arrive in Karlova."

"You must tell them I will not do it. I want to get to know the man whose wife I have to be. It would be crazy to marry anyone without knowing him first."

She was aware that her uncle could not think of an answer and she kissed him on the cheek and sighed,

"Never mind, we have been lucky so far and let's hope that we will continue to be lucky in the future."

She moved away and had no idea that, as his eyes followed her, there was an extremely worried look in them.

But he could not tell Tarena that all he had heard so far of Prince Igor had not been in any way complimentary.

CHAPTER THREE

At Athens the Ambassador had gone ashore to visit his Embassy there and sign the visitor's book at others.

When he came back to the Battleship, he waited until he was alone with the Earl before telling him that the current situation was becoming extremely worrying.

"Why particularly?" the Earl enquired.

They were sitting together on deck and as Tarena and the Count were playing deck tennis, there was no one to overhear them.

Even so the Ambassador lowered his voice as he began,

"The Russians are not only causing trouble outside their country especially in the Balkans, but they are having revolutionary difficulties of their own in St. Petersburg."

The Earl raised his eyebrows.

"Well, they had the same problems under the last Czar, who they eventually destroyed."

"Alexander III is a hard man in more ways than one," added the Ambassador. "He is strong physically, which is why he was able to save his family when the revolutionaries blew up the train he was in."

"I have not heard about that, Your Excellency. Is it possible he will meet the same fate as his father?"

"He may well do. Apparently the Imperial train on its way from the Caucasus went off the rails near the town of Borki."

"It sounds extremely worrying!"

"The Czarina and the Czar were having luncheon with their children in the dining car. The roof caved in and the floor buckled as the carriage fell headlong onto its side. For once the Emperor's Herculean strength proved itself worthy of the occasion."

"What happened then?" the Earl enquired.

"By brute force he freed his wife and children from the wreck of the coach and servants and nannies climbed out through the window."

"I have never heard anything so awful!"

The Earl was wondering, if that sort of thing was going on in Russia itself, what might happen in Karlova.

After a moment he reflected,

"Well, if Czar Alexander has to try and cope with all these revolutionaries at home, he may not be so anxious to pursue the Russian menace abroad."

"Unfortunately, I was told at the Embassy that his ambition has not been diminished. He burns with endless indignation at the thought that Russia might have failed in her mission to dominate the Balkans."

"We are aware of that, but I hoped that the new Czar would have more sense than his predecessor."

"What he is doing is very subtle. As he cannot afford another war, he keeps his troops at home. In fact some of the more naïve Statesmen have already referred to him as *The Czar Peacemaker*."

"Then they must be exceedingly stupid," the Earl murmured almost beneath his breath.

"What his Foreign Minister, de Giers, is doing," the Ambassador said, "is to encourage Russian revolutionaries to act as *agents provocateurs* to stir up trouble for the established regimes of the Balkans.

"I am told that Russian agents are posing as icon-sellers and spreading all over the Balkan countries to set up subversive cells. The Russian Embassy officials even pay large crowds to stage riots."

"Can they really be doing all this?" the Earl asked.

It seemed to him that the Ambassador had been extremely alarmed by all he had heard in Athens and he tried to hope that he was now exaggerating the story.

"I have been told," the Ambassador went on, "that Russian Officers in the Eastern Rumelian part of Bulgaria have opened gymnasiums where they train boys and girls in guerrilla warfare."

"I really don't believe it," the Earl exclaimed.

"I do wish I had your optimism, my Lord."

"The Russians have had some setbacks. Equally it has been proved over and over again that only the British Union Jack over a Palace guarantees a certain amount of safety and peace for the occupants."

There was silence between the two men before the Ambassador added,

"There was another matter I learnt while I was in Athens, which I think I must warn my Government about when I reach home."

"What is that?" the Earl asked him, feeling much more worried about Tarena that he had been before.

How could she possibly cope, as her father would have done, with the Russians doing everything they could think of to make and incite trouble?

And with being married to a man she had not yet met?

"The Russians," the Ambassador was saying, "are determined to promote revolutions in the Balkans as soon as they can."

"We have heard that before, but I can only hope that Karlova will be strong and can depend on their armed forces to watch out for those disgusting turncoats who are always prepared to go where there is money."

"There I agree with you, my Lord. It is whispered that the Russian Intelligence Service in the Balkans is more than prepared to spend very large sums of money on those who will work for them."

"I am surprised they have so much cash."

When the conversation was over, the Earl felt his head was in a whirl.

He was now even more concerned than he had been before about the future for Tarena.

'How can she possibly survive?' he asked himself. 'Unless Prince Igor is really clever and will understand and deal with the country's problems before the revolutionaries can actually establish a hold on the country.'

He thought he might say something to Tarena.

Yet he knew that he must be very careful not to prejudice her against the man she was to marry or indeed against Karlova itself before they actually arrived.

*

Because she was so fond of her uncle and they had always been so close, Tarena knew without being told that he was worried.

"What is upsetting you, Uncle Richard?" she asked. "I know there is something occupying you, because there is a little frown on your forehead that is only there when you are anticipating that something unpleasant will happen."

The Earl laughed.

"Now you are disturbing me, Tarena, but I am, of course, if I am totally honest, worrying about you and the difficulties you will face as Queen."

"Then I think I must leave anything to do with the Russians to my husband when I have one. Another thing that really horrifies me is that the new Czar is so cruel to the Jews."

"Who has been talking to you about that?"

"Actually I read about it in one of the newspapers we bought in Athens. It said that the new Czar's reign opened with a persecution of the Jews which has surpassed that in any other country."

She gave a little sigh before she added,

"After all, no one can help how they are born. It's not fair that people should be persecuted and killed because their rulers don't like the blood in their veins."

"I agree with you, my dearest, and I did hear that thousands of Jews have been murdered and their property confiscated."

"Surely someone must have protested against such cruelty. What happened to the Jewish children?"

"I think a great number of them survived."

It seemed, as *The Royal Sovereign* steamed nearer to Karlova, as if the problems that Tarena would have to face as soon as she became Queen became more and more forbidding day by day.

The Earl could only pray to God, as he had prayed already, that Prince Igor, who had lived in the Balkans all his life, would be able to save Karlova from the Russian menace.

But he fully recognised that the only real asset they had to protect and save them was the blessing of Queen Victoria in the guise of Tarena herself.

Their arrival in one of the latest and largest British Battleships would surely impress anyone, especially those Karlovans who were contemplating rebellion.

He could understand Tarena's desire to get to know Prince Igor before she married him.

Yet to wait might be a danger to the people over whom she was to reign.

"Now tell me, Uncle Richard," Tarena was asking, "why you are so worried at this particular moment. Is it because you heard bad news about Karlova while we were in Athens?"

The Earl thought that, with her quick brain and her undoubted knowledge of current affairs, she would not easily be deceived.

"All Embassies are inclined to give one bad news rather than good and, as you already know, all the Balkan countries with access to the Aegean Sea are particularly prized by the Russians."

"In other words, Uncle Richard, we are more likely to be attacked than Principalities situated further inland?"

"Of course. It is something which has been known in England for a long time. That is why Her Majesty is so keen to place the crown on your head and have a stalwart King by your side."

Tarena made a little murmur, but she did not speak and he continued,

"That will fully demonstrate to the Russians that the Union Jack is a very valuable asset and a prize they cannot steal, however much they scheme and plot."

Tarena laughed, as he meant her to do.

"I do like the way you put it, but I have read the newspapers and things appear to be very difficult in Russia itself at the moment."

The Earl nodded to show that he agreed.

"I cannot imagine why, Uncle Richard, when they are so large and powerful already, they should bother about a small Kingdom like Karlova."

"The greedy are always greedy, and it will be your job, Tarena, to keep them well outside your frontiers. And to make sure that any Russian who does infiltrate into Karlova is quickly thrown out before he can do any harm."

"You make it sound simple, Uncle Richard, but if you are worried, I know the Count is worried too, although he is too tactful to say so to me."

*

That evening after dinner she and the Count went on deck.

It was a lovely night and *The Royal Sovereign* was moving into a quiet bay, so that they could sleep peacefully without the disturbance of the engines.

There was a moon rising up in the sky and the stars were coming out one by one.

"It is *so* beautiful," Tarena sighed softly.

"And so are you," the Count added gently. "Far too beautiful for any man's peace of mind."

Tarena turned and smiled at him.

"That is the nicest compliment you could have ever paid me, Count Vladimir."

"Surely you understand that I am trying not to tell you how beautiful you are and how I lie awake at night thinking of you, so I am unable to sleep."

He spoke almost harshly as if he was trying to fight against her.

"I am sorry if I do that to you. Naturally you know how important it has been for me to have you with me and to learn from you so much about the country I have to rule over."

"Karlova is the most fortunate country in the world because they will have you, but I am desperately afraid that you will find it too difficult."

The Count paused for a moment and then he added reflectively,

"I just could not bear to see you disillusioned and unhappy."

"Why should I be so?" Tarena questioned him.

He did not answer and after a moment, she probed him further,

"I have a distinct feeling that you don't think I will be happy with Prince Igor."

"I have not said so and it most certainly is not my business to interfere," the Count replied hastily. "But I sincerely want you to be happy and, as I have just said, I don't want you to be upset by anyone in Karlova."

Tarena was silent for a moment and then she said, gazing out at the silvery sea,

"I have always dreamed that one day I would meet someone with whom I would fall in love and be as happy as my Papa and Mama were. Everyone has told me – my uncle, the servants and everyone who knew them – that they were so much in love that for them the world was Heaven because they were together – "

Her voice seemed to die away into the soft lap of the waves.

"Do you suppose I don't want that for you too?" the Count asked. "I want you to be happy, so blissfully happy that you will never regret leaving England and coming to a place where to you everyone is a stranger."

"Although I have never seen them, they are my people because they were Papa's – "

"You are right, Your Royal Highness. You belong to them, as they belong to you, and because we bear the same name and the same blood, I also in my own way belong to you."

Tarena turned and smiled at him.

"Of course you do, Count Vladimir. You have the same name as Papa and we are cousins. So you cannot fail to help me in what is going to be the biggest task I have ever undertaken in my life."

"I will help you in every way I can," the Count said. "I am prepared to dedicate my whole life not only to keeping you safe but keeping you happy."

"That is a lovely thing to say!" Tarena exclaimed. "If everyone in Karlova is as kind as you have been to me, then I will be very happy and will not feel homesick for England."

"You must promise me one thing."

"What is that?" she asked.

"If you want anything, however difficult, however strange, you will ask me. Somehow, in some way, I will find it for you, even if it will mean climbing the highest mountain or diving to the very bottom of the sea."

Tarena clapped her hands together.

"Now you are being poetic. We will, I feel sure, thwart the Russians together. When they see your soldiers and my crown, they will all run away!"

She was making it a game and the Count chuckled.

"You are turning it into a Fairy story and that is exactly what it will be. You will be the Fairy Queen, more exciting and more glamorous than any Queen has ever been before."

"I should like that," Tarena sighed.

There was a short silence before she said in a small voice,

"But I have not yet met Prince Igor."

"He will, I am sure, be waiting for you when you arrive tomorrow afternoon."

"As soon as that? It may seem wrong of me, but I don't want to leave *The Royal Sovereign* so quickly. I do wish we could go on perhaps into the Black Sea or better still to India, which I have always wanted to visit."

"I have been there, Your Royal Highness, and I know you would find it as fascinating as I did."

The Count paused before he said in a voice she could hardly hear,

"Perhaps one day we can go there together."

"But, of course, why not?" Tarena cried. "A Royal Visit with these delightful people we have on board now. I am sure the Viceroy would be only too pleased."

The Count did not answer her and she mused that perhaps he had been thinking of a less formal visit.

'It would be such fun,' she thought, 'if it was at all possible. Yet perhaps Prince Igor, whatever he is like, would refuse to leave Karlova.'

She had wished when they departed from Athens that they had been able to stop at all the Greek Islands, but the Ambassador had insisted again how vital it was that they should arrive as rapidly as possible.

There was no chance of Tarena going ashore at Delos where Apollo had been born.

She had read everything she could find about the Greek Islands and to her they were the most glamorous and exciting islands in the whole world.

But she only had a brief glimpse of some of them as they steamed past.

She had thought that perhaps one day she would be able to come back and then go ashore and muse of what they meant to the Greeks in their literature and in their imagination.

After a moment, as the anchor ran down and *The Royal Sovereign* came to a standstill, Tarena sighed,

"As we are now approaching Karlova, this is the last night when I will be able to look up at the moon and the stars as I am doing just now and talk to you, Count Vladimir."

"I would hope you will often want to talk to me, as I am in charge of your Royal Bodyguard at the Palace, but perhaps it will not be in such a private place and we may never be alone."

Tarena looked at him and then she said quickly,

"You are not suggesting that I will have to take a Lady-in-Waiting with me everywhere I go or that it would be wrong for you and me ever to be alone together?"

"It is something I want more than I want anything in the whole world. But protocol is protocol in the Palace. For the Queen to be found alone with the Captain of her Bodyguard would undoubtedly cause undesirable gossip and speculation."

"But you are my cousin, Count Vladimir, and when my Uncle Richard goes home, there will be no one I can confide in to if I am not able to talk to you."

"You will have your husband," the Count replied in a hard voice.

"But it would not be the same as talking to you," Tarena protested. "After all, we are blood relatives and there is no one else I can speak to as freely as I have been able to talk to you ever since we met."

She gave a little laugh before she added,

"I feel as if I have known you all my life."

"And I feel the same, but because you are to be Queen and I am of no consequence, I must not do anything that will seem wrong in the eyes of those who are watching you constantly."

"Watching me?" Tarena questioned.

"Just remember that if you need me, I am always there," he continued as if she had not spoken. "And if I am not at your side, as I long to be, it will just be because I am putting my duty in front of my adoration for you."

"*Now* you are frightening me, Count Vladimir. Oh, why must I be placed on a pedestal and not allowed to be human any longer?"

"You will be Queen, and Queens do not, if they are wise, spend any time with insignificant young men. Above all, you must not tempt me. You know I want to be with you and we have a great deal to say to each other, but when we arrive, I must sink into the background and you have to pretend that you don't notice me."

Tarena gave a little cry and turned away to lean over the rail once again.

"Now you are being cruel and unkind. Of course, I am intimidated by what may lie ahead, but I am trying to be brave about it. At the same time I very much wish that we could turn round and go back to England – now."

The Count came nearer to her.

"I don't want you to feel like that," he said. "I want you to feel it is a great adventure and that you are doing something noble in helping people who are really helpless against the Russians, unless they are led and given the will to fight for their rightful independence."

"I want – to do that," Tarena murmured. "But you are the only one when Uncle Richard goes home who will understand what I am feeling and realise how difficult the whole situation is."

"I will be there," the Count persisted. "But I am trying to make you realise that your husband must come first in your thoughts, your feelings *and* your heart."

There was silence for what seemed a long time.

Then Tarena stuttered in a repressed voice he could hardly hear,

"Suppose – I do not – like him."

"But you will, you must! Karlova has to have a King and there is no one else."

"Why is there no one else?" Tarena asked.

"Because, as you well know, your father and Queen Catrina did not produce any children and with the one exception of Prince Igor of Dubnik himself there is no other Royalty in the whole country."

"What about your family?"

The Count smiled.

"I wish I had one. My father, who was of course a Sazon and went to England on a visit when he was a young man, actually found some gold in our mountains which has never been developed."

Tarena was listening wide-eyed as he continued,

"I have mentioned it once or twice to members of the Cabinet, but they have always claimed that it was not worthwhile investigating the find further."

"But I feel strongly that it should be investigated," Tarena asserted. "After all, if the country had more money they could expand and re-equip the Army and Navy and put up a really strong resistance against the Russians."

"Exactly what I said, but no one listened to me."

"So after your father left England, he came home?" Tarena questioned the Count.

"Yes. He fell in love with a girl who belonged to one of the oldest and most distinguished families in the country, which has now dwindled away over the years until I am almost the only member left."

"But a very nice member and a very kind member – who will look after me – "

"I promise I will and perhaps one day we will go exploring and find the gold my father discovered and use it to make Karlova a far more prosperous country."

"That is a wonderful idea, which I will not forget. We must talk about it, so you will have to come and see me regularly even if I am sitting on an uncomfortable throne!"

The Count chuckled.

"I will try to make it comfortable for you, though I don't think that gold is particularly nice to sit on!"

They both laughed and then the Count suggested,

"You will have to look really beautiful tomorrow, especially when you make your all-important speech to all those who are welcoming you. Therefore I think that you should retire now, Your Royal Highness."

Tarena sighed.

"I would so much rather stay here talking to you. Promise me by everything you hold sacred that you will not disappear when we arrive at Karlova, but will stay by me and watch over me."

"I swear to you on my honour that I will do so until you are married to Prince Igor. Then, if I find that life has become unbearable for me, I will go gold-digging on my own."

"You are not to," protested Tarena. "It would be unfair. You have told me about it and if ever you do go gold-digging then I want to come too!"

"It would not be very easy for a woman to take part in it. Anyway this is only dream-talk. We would need so much money to invest. In fact I know that it cost my father almost everything he possessed. But the sheer realisation that he had found gold was always the delight and triumph of his life."

"Promise you will not go without me – "

Tarena looked up at him as she spoke.

As their eyes met again, they were both very still.

Then, as if he forced himself to do so, the Count took her hand and raised it to his lips.

"I promise you anything and everything you could ever possibly desire – Your Royal Highness."

Without waiting for a reply, the Count walked away leaving her alone in the moonlight.

She watched him until he was out of sight.

It was only when she climbed into bed that Tarena mused that their conversation had been a very strange one.

It was one she did not really understand.

She only knew she was now more frightened of what lay ahead than she had been at the beginning of the voyage.

It was not at what had been openly said, but she knew that after stopping at Athens her uncle had spent a long time with the Ambassador.

She had then known instinctively, because they had always been so close, that he was extremely worried.

The newspapers had made it very clear that she was going into danger.

It had been one thing to read all about the Russian's dastardly interest in the Balkans when she was so far away in England and it had nothing to do with her.

Now it was very different.

Tomorrow she would enter a country that was high on the Russian's list for taking over and exploitation.

The mere idea that she – a young girl – could keep them at bay was really laughable.

In fact it seemed incredible that Queen Victoria and anyone else in England had thought it at all possible.

Tarena had always prayed with her uncle and the God he worshipped had always seemed very real to her.

So before she got into bed she prayed fervently that life in Karlova would not be as terrifying as looked likely at the moment.

She was not really afraid of dying.

She believed, as her uncle did, that her mother and father were waiting for her in Heaven.

She had been sent out to save the people of Karlova from the Russians, but she was afraid of being completely ineffective and letting the country fall into their hands.

'Help me, God. Oh, please, help me,' she prayed. 'Make the Count see that he must be with me, because if he is not, I will have no one to talk to. No one will understand as he does why I am here and why I am trying to do what my father did for his people who all trusted him. *Please*, please help me.'

When she finally climbed into her bed, she found it impossible to sleep.

She lay thinking how beautiful the moonlight had been and the kind words the Count had said to her.

She could not help feeling that he too was suffering in some way.

She had a sudden feeling of horror about tomorrow and the people who would be waiting to meet her when she arrived.

They could hardly expect a young girl of eighteen to be their bulwark against the sturdy Russian guns, the Russian intrigues and the Russian Secret Service.

She could feel them all rising up like ogres in front of her and there was only herself with her small hands to prevent them from conquering the country and making it part of their great Empire.

'I cannot do it, I will fail utterly,' she thought again frantically.

Then, just as she had felt when she had made the decision to go to Karlova, she sensed that her father was calling to her again and so was her mother.

They were standing hand in hand and smiling in a radiant light that seemed to envelope them.

They were telling her gently not to be afraid.

They were both watching over her and she was not alone.

'Help me! Please help me!' she wanted to cry out again to them.

Already they were saying, she realised, that she was under their protection now and for always.

And, although it seemed incredible, that she would win the great battle she was setting out to fight.

No one, not even the Russians would be able to stop her.

When she finally fell asleep, she slept peacefully and dreamlessly.

*

When she woke up in the morning, she remembered exactly how she had felt the night before.

How she had been made to feel completely certain that her father and mother were with her.

She was interrupted in her reveries by the Baroness who opened the door of her cabin and called out,

"I don't want to hurry you, Your Royal Highness, but the Captain tells me that we will be in Port within three-quarters of an hour and your breakfast is waiting for you."

Tarena jumped out of bed.

"What did I decide I was going to wear today?" she asked more of herself than the Baroness. "I want to look pretty but impressive. I just cannot remember which dress I chose."

"Let me help you," the Baroness offered. "You are quite right, Your Royal Highness has to look particularly splendid today. But I am sure you will find the whole City is waiting to welcome you and longing for you to be as good a Queen as your father was our King."

Tarena did not answer.

She was recalling again how her father had come to her last night and she was sure whatever she said or did he would be helping and guiding her.

She found the dress she had chosen the day before hanging up in the corner of the cabin and the rest of her clothes had already been packed.

She dressed quickly and when she appeared in the cabin where the rest of the party were breakfasting, her uncle exclaimed,

"You look lovely, Tarena! That dress and hat are exactly what I would have chosen if you had asked me!"

"I remember now, although I had forgotten it this morning, that you particularly admired this dress when we bought it together in Bond Street, Uncle Richard."

"Did your charming uncle really help you with your trousseau?" the Ambassador's wife asked.

"He chose most of it for me, insisting that he knew exactly how I ought to look, while I was too modest to manage it myself."

They all laughed and Tarena continued,

"I personally thought I would look more impressive if I arrived wearing my wedding dress and a grand tiara, but

I will keep that for the next step, which I am hoping will not happen too quickly after I arrive."

She caught an expression on the Ambassador's face and knew that was what he was intending.

'I will not do it, I will not!' she said to herself as she sat down at the table. 'I only hope that Prince Igor is thinking the same as I am, and is determined that we will become friends before we are made man and wife.'

It was something she dared not say aloud.

As the Ambassador's wife and the Baroness talked excitedly of what had been planned for them tonight, she was silent.

It was only about a quarter of an hour later when one of the Officers came into the room, saluted stiffly and announced,

"The Captain has asked me to inform Your Royal Highness that we will be moving into Port in the next ten minutes."

The Ambassador's wife and the Baroness jumped to their feet. They had come down to breakfast without their hats and they ran to their cabins to retrieve them.

Tarena was completely ready. She had only to pick up her handbag before she stepped ashore.

"You are not scared, my dearest?" her uncle asked her in a whisper.

She slipped her hand into his.

"I am terrified that I will do something wrong, but I am so happy that you are here and so I am not alone."

"You know I would not allow that, Tarena."

"Do you think Prince Igor will be waiting for me as we dock, Uncle Richard?"

"I have no idea, but I expect the Prime Minister will be there and the most senior Members of the Cabinet. He will make a speech, which I hope you will understand and I expect Count Vladimir has told you how to thank them."

"Yes indeed, he has helped me write my speech in Karlovan and I do want to say goodbye and thank you to his soldiers before we go ashore."

"I think that will be difficult, because they will land before we do to take up their positions round the platform where you will be speaking."

As Tarena was about to protest, he added,

"Don't forget you will see them later at the Palace, where they are posted with many other troops to look after you and guard you under the Count's command."

Tarena did not answer.

She thought to herself that everything would be all right and safe if the Count was there.

If she failed to carry out all the instructions he had given her, he would be on hand to prompt her.

"You are not to be frightened, my dearest Tarena," her uncle was insisting. "After all, these people loved your father and I am absolutely certain they will love you too."

"I hope so, Uncle Richard," Tarena sighed.

Then she slipped her hand into his as the Battleship shuddered to a halt on the dockside.

CHAPTER FOUR

Tarena's heart was beating violently as she walked onto the deck holding her uncle's hand tightly.

Just below she could see a huge crowd of people.

At the front of the quay there was a small platform with a number of men standing on it.

They were all smartly dressed for the occasion and she guessed that they must be the Prime Minister and other officials.

There were only men on the platform.

And there were mostly men in the crowd.

They did not cheer.

As she then reached the platform and its occupants bowed to her, a band she had not noticed before burst into the Karlovan National Anthem.

Everyone stood to attention.

Then the man she gathered was the Prime Minister asked her to move forward and they stood for a few moments at the front of the platform so the crowd could see her.

The Prime Minister murmured the names, that she had difficulty in hearing, of the members of the deputation and who bowed individually as he did so.

It was obvious that Prince Igor was not there and she gave a little sigh of relief.

She was then invited to sit down, followed by the rest of the official party.

The Prime Minister then went into a long address welcoming her to the country as their Queen.

The Prime Minister's speech was most flattering about her father and fortunately she was able to understand most of it.

He spoke of their deep gratitude to her that she had taken up the position he had left empty – and that now, in their eyes, she was already the Queen of Karlova.

He prophesied that she would live to be a great age and provide the country with heirs to the throne that had sadly been lacking in the recent past.

When he finally came to a close, the men on the platform applauded.

However, Tarena was well aware that none of the crowd listening and watching made any movement.

It was then that she took a deep breath and looked round quickly to see if Count Vladimir was beside her.

She faced, not the Prime Minister and the officials with him, but the people on the quayside who were staring at her in what she felt was a somewhat hostile manner and she could not help feeling that they were not really all that pleased to see her.

They were perhaps thinking that because she was a woman, even though she was her father's daughter, that she would be a failure and unable to protect them.

She had learnt by heart an ingratiating and effusive speech that had been put together for her by the Count and he had rehearsed every word with her over and over again, so that she was word perfect.

She was to say how much she was looking forward to taking her father's place on the throne of Karlova.

How she promised to carry on everything he had achieved during his reign.

And how she sincerely hoped that Karlova would be an example to the other countries of the Balkans.

Instead she gazed at the assembly of men staring at her somewhat morosely.

Suddenly Tarena felt a surging wave of confidence and determination sweep through her body as if she was being directed from another world.

She threw both her arms into the air in a dramatic gesture and began to speak in strong firm voice,

"Fellow Karlovans! I need your help! I have come here because, as I know, my father reigned here in peace and happiness and loved you all as you loved him. But I have always lived in England, and I am very worried that I may fail you, and may not rule the country as you want it ruled.

"So you have to help me. I know I am a woman, but I have my father's blood in my veins and I knew when they first asked me to come here that he was guiding me, as he is indeed guiding me now."

Her voice rang out so that everyone could hear her clearly and to her great surprise her Karlovan was fluent and without any hesitation.

She felt as if the men watching her came alive and began to respond to her words.

"The future is not going to be easy for any of us," she went on. "You know better than I do what a dangerous situation this country is in. But we have to save it and we can only do so if you and I work closely together."

She looked round at them and continued,

"You must tell me what you think and what you want, and make it very clear from the beginning. It is *you* who are important and it is *you* who are this wonderful country. We must fight not only with our bodies but with our brains to keep Karlova independent and free."

Now there was a distant murmur from the crowd and Tarena could only pray that it was one of approval.

She threw out her arms again,

"Help me! Help me! Come to me individually and speak to me in the Palace and tell me what you think. I would rather hear from you than from anyone else, because it is you I represent, you who will place the Crown on my head and you who will make me your Queen. Only if we work together can we remain, as we are now, an example to the Balkans and even to the world beyond."

As Tarena finished, she bowed to them.

After a moment's astonished pause, a man in the crowd shouted out,

"I knew your father and fine man he were too."

He was standing close to the platform with only a few men in front of him.

To everyone's amazement Tarena jumped down on to the quayside and walked purposively towards the man.

As she reached him, she held out her hand saying,

"You knew my father? Tell me about him and how much he meant to you and what did he do for you?"

The man who was obviously a workman, took her hand in his and said,

"I said he were a fine man and you be fine for a woman. We'll try to help you, if that's what you wants."

"It is what I want and what I pray you will give me," Tarena replied.

She next turned to the men around her and held out her hand.

She shook the hands of dozens of them, as those at the back tried to push up to the front to get closer to her.

She did not look back, but the Prime Minister and all on the platform were watching her with astonishment.

Some of them were muttering that nothing like this had ever been done before in Karlova.

Only the Count had followed her.

Behind him were two soldiers, the others were still on guard round the platform.

In half-an-hour Tarena had shaken hands with most of the crowd and talked to those who wanted to speak to her about her father.

It was then she heard the Count's voice saying,

"The carriage is a little way ahead of you, Your Royal Highness, and I think you should now go to it."

"Very well, Count Vladimir," Tarena replied.

Then she stopped to speak to one of the few women who had come to the quayside.

She had two small boys with her and Tarena bent down to pat their cheeks and told their mother what good-looking children they were.

"We never expected you to be quite like this," the woman said, "and perhaps like your father you'll bring us peace and quiet."

"That is what I intend to do," Tarena told her. "Ask the other women to come to the Palace and tell me what they want done for themselves and their children."

The woman's eyes lit up.

"We need some better schools for one thing," she said, "and we has to walk ten miles to go to a hospital."

"Then what we must do is to build a hospital here in the City. And I will see if I can improve the schools."

The woman gave a shriek of delight.

It was then that Tarena felt the Count touch her arm and move her swiftly towards the carriage.

It was an open one, drawn by four white horses and the coachman and footman on the box wore an attractive and bright livery.

When she stepped into the carriage, she found to her delight her uncle was already sitting there.

There was a surge forward by the crowd that had followed her up the quayside until she reached the carriage and she could see, as she looked back, most of the officials on the platform were already in carriages behind her.

The Count climbed in just before the horses moved off to sit with his back to them.

As the carriage moved away, the crowd cheered and Tarena waved until they were out of sight.

Then she gave a little sigh and sat back onto the upholstered eat as she looked towards her uncle.

"Was I alright?" she asked a little apprehensively.

"You were brilliant, absolutely brilliant," the Count exclaimed before the Earl could speak. "Never before has any Royal walked as you did into the crowd, shaking them by the hand and being as one might say *familiar*. This really does open up a new chapter for Kings and Queens."

The Count looked at the Earl and asked,

"Am I not right in saying that, my Lord?"

"I had no idea that Tarena would do such a thing, but it was certainly very effective. I had a feeling when we stepped ashore that the majority of the men there were hostile towards us."

"You are quite right. The Russians have been very busy among the men who work in the Port. As you may have seen, there were practically no women there."

"I noticed that," the Earl replied. "I thought myself until Tarena went down amongst them that they intended to give us a very cold reception."

"I feel from what I heard, as I was following her, that they intended to start a hostile demonstration of their dislike of being ruled by a woman – in fact of being ruled at all."

Tarena drew in her breath, as the Count carried on,

"I will learn more later from my men who have been here all the time I was away. I knew when I saw the crowd at the quayside that we might be in for trouble."

The horses were now gathering speed.

Although there were a good number of people in the streets watching them as they passed, there were not the masses the Count had hoped for.

Tarena knew from the expressions on their faces that both her uncle and the Count were worried.

*

The Palace was even more beautiful than she had expected.

It was at the far end of the City and had been built on slightly higher ground and, when the horses came to a standstill, there was a flight of white marble steps leading up to the Palace which itself was dazzling white.

With the sun shining onto the windows it looked more like a Fairy Palace than Tarena had anticipated.

There were huge fountains playing on either side of the marble steps and there was a profusion of blossom on the shrubs that bordered the gardens.

"It is *so* lovely," Tarena sighed in a somewhat awed voice to her uncle.

"I am admiring it too," he replied.

"I have been thinking that it is a perfect background for you," the Count said to Tarena. "And may I say once again that you have made your début in a most unusual and surprising fashion, which I am quite certain, will change the whole mood of the City."

As he spoke, he turned and looked back and Tarena asked him quickly,

"What can you see?"

"I should not be surprised if we are now being followed by a number of the men who were on the quay and many others who have been told of your unexpected behaviour on arrival."

Tarena laughed.

"You make it sound awful."

"It was so clever of you," the Count cried. "I only wish I had thought of it myself."

He was not just paying her compliments to reassure her and she knew by the expression in his eyes that he was telling her the truth.

He was simply delighted at the entrance she had made into Karlova.

Next they climbed up the marble steps and Tarena wondered if Prince Igor would be waiting at the top.

Instead there was only the Lord Chamberlain, who introduced himself, and there were many equerries.

They too were a little surprised when she shook each of them by the hand.

Then the Lord Chamberlain announced that there were refreshments waiting for them in the dining room.

"I am certainly very thirsty!" Tarena exclaimed. "I would also like to wash my hands after having had them shaken by so many rather dirty ones."

The Lord Chamberlain stared at her.

"Dirty hands! How could you have encountered those, Your Royal Highness?"

There was a twinkle in the Count's eyes as he said,

"Her Royal Highness insisted on meeting all the people on the quayside who were there to welcome her.

She must have spoken to at least two or three hundred of them and shaken them by the hand."

"*Spoken to them*," the Lord Chamberlain repeated as if he had not understood what the Count was saying.

"Unless I am very much mistaken, the City will be talking of nothing else tonight. In fact I think, my Lord, you should be prepared for a great number of visitors in the next hour or so who will want to see Her Royal Highness again to be absolutely certain they were not dreaming!"

"I think *I* am doing the dreaming, if I understand what you are saying," the Lord Chamberlain replied.

Count Vladimir chuckled.

Then the Prime Minister and his party arrived.

They went into the dining room where there were a number of others who had come earlier. Many of them were the wives of Members of the Cabinet.

It was impossible for the time being for Tarena to leave, as so many wanted to be introduced to her.

Finally, because she was hot and there seemed no end to those coming into the room, she took off her hat.

She put it down on a chair and pushed her curls into place and she had no idea that she was doing anything wrong or unusual.

Every woman in the room was wearing a hat and they were staring at Tarena in disbelief.

The Count's eyes were twinkling as he realised how surprised some of them were.

There were refreshments of every sort on the table and, as it was impossible to serve everyone crowding into the Palace, the guests were asked to help themselves.

The servants were wearing, Tarena thought, a very attractive livery and they poured out champagne.

The Count brought her a glass.

"It's no use going away to tidy up," he said. "If you disappear, everyone will merely think you were part of a dream and they will go home disappointed!"

Tarena knew that he was teasing her.

She laughed and taking the champagne from him, she declared,

"I am certainly thirsty, but I am so glad you are not angry with me for not using the speech you wrote for me."

"Only you could have thought of anything quite so brilliant and so brave," he replied "and which has never been done before."

"Is that really true?" Tarena asked him.

"You could hardly expect to see Queen Victoria shaking hands in a crowd like you have just enchanted."

They both laughed.

It was impossible to say more because the Prime Minister brought up yet another distinguished personage to meet their new Queen.

It was an hour later when the Count came to say,

"There is a huge crowd gathering outside who want to see you. Are you brave enough to go down and wave to them?"

"Of course, Count Vladimir. But you and Uncle Richard had better come along with me, unless you think I should take the Prime Minister."

"I think the Prime Minister is astonished enough about what is happening. As I have no idea what you will do or say, I think if your uncle and I walk on either side of you, we can keep you in order!"

Tarena giggled.

When she moved towards the door, the Earl, as if he was aware of what was happening, followed her.

It was only when they went outside the front door of the Palace and looked down that they saw hundreds of people outside the gates.

It was only because sentries were on guard that they did not burst through them.

Without her hat or gloves, Tarena started to walk down the marble steps with the two men on either side.

When she reached the bottom step, she saw that the people were already cheering and waving outside the gates.

She could now see that there were a good number of small children and their mothers with them.

The men on the whole, she thought, looked slightly better dressed than those who had been waiting for her on the quay.

The soldiers presented arms at her appearance and the Officer in charge looked at her as if for instructions.

"Open the gates," Tarena ordered bravely.

"Open the gates, Your Royal Highness?" queried the Officer as if he could not have heard her correctly.

"I want the people to see me, which they cannot do where they are. And I want to talk to them."

Neither her uncle nor the Count made any protest and the Officer ordered his soldiers to open the gates.

Tarena was standing a little higher than the people outside and she began to address them,

"Thank you for coming to see me. I think perhaps you would like to shake me by the hand and give me your good wishes. As I have already told the people on the quay when I arrived, I need your help, everyone of you, to make our country not only happy but prosperous and free. I can only do it if every man, woman and child, helps me."

She paused before she added,

"So please give me not only your help, but your love. I can do nothing without it."

They all cheered at these words.

"As I want to meet as many of you as possible, will you please come in and shake me by the hand and then come further in and sit down on the grass."

There was a startled gasp from the Officer.

Tarena bent forward to shake hands with an elderly man, who piped up,

"You be a chip off the old block and that's what we needs here in Karlova."

"Thank you, kind sir. Now sit down on the grass, that I am sure is quite dry, then the others will understand that is what they have to do as well."

The old man and two others understood.

They shook her by the hand, each of them saying something pleasant and then passed by and moved onto the grass on either side of the steps and sat down.

In quite a short time the lawns were packed with people and the children were delighted with the fountains.

There was still a crowd coming up the road to take part in this unprecedented scene.

It was the Count who finally suggested,

"I think Your Royal Highness has done enough. I therefore propose that you walk up the steps and when you reach the top, just disappear, then the people will gradually disperse and go home."

"There is hardly room for any more anyway. And my hand, because they will squeeze it so hard, is almost falling off!"

"I was afraid it would be, but you have been so magnificent, utterly and completely magnificent. It will change the whole thinking of the City."

"What were they thinking before?" asked Tarena.

"I have a suspicion that the Russians have been busy while I was away," the Count said in a whisper. "But we will talk more about it later."

Tarena felt he was quite right that where they were was not the right place for a private conversation.

She climbed up a few more steps and waved to the people below and on either side of her.

"I am now going to have my tea," she said. "But will you please come and see me another day? If you have anything of great importance to discuss with me, leave a note here at the Palace and I will try to get in touch with you as soon as possible."

Those sitting on the grass were for the moment too spellbound to open their mouths.

Then, as Tarena started to walk up the rest of the steps, they all cheered.

When she reached the top step, she turned round to wave and, as the crowd waved back at her, she went into the Palace.

The Lord Chamberlain was waiting in the doorway.

"Such an event has never happened before, Your Royal Highness," he told her nervously. "The people have never been allowed inside the gates."

"Well, there has to be a first time for everything," she answered. "I think you will agree they have behaved very well and they are already moving away quietly."

She looked back and the Lord Chamberlain noted that the women with children were going out through the gates into the road.

As Tarena walked to the room where the guests were still enjoying refreshments, the Lord Chamberlain turned to Count Vladimir,

"Is this one of your wild ideas?"

"Not guilty, my Lord," the Count replied. "It was entirely spontaneous and something Her Royal Highness had not even thought of doing when we disembarked."

"I don't know what the world is coming to. I have certainly never seen anything like this before – "

The Count smiled.

"I think you will see a great deal more of it in the future. If you ask me, she is going to save Karlova."

In the dining room, the guests, who had not realised what was happening outside, were laughing and talking amongst themselves and enjoying the champagne.

At last the guests began to go and they were all determined to say something different to their new Queen.

It was then the Earl said in a low voice to the Lord Chamberlain,

"Where is Prince Igor? I had expected him to be here to greet us."

"It is what I expected too," the Lord Chamberlain replied. "I sent a messenger to notify him three days ago of the time that the Battleship would arrive, but there has been no reply."

"It seems to me quite extraordinary and, if you will forgive me for saying so, extremely rude."

"I agree with you. I have never met Prince Igor, but I have heard he is a very peculiar man with ideas of his own."

The Lord Chamberlain paused for a moment before he added,

"Because he lives quite some distance from here, he seldom comes to the City."

"I can understand that, but I gather you are very anxious to have the wedding and the Coronation as soon as possible."

"I think if you ask the Prime Minister, he is still determined that it should take place in two days time," the Lord Chamberlain replied.

The Earl frowned.

He knew that Tarena was understandably anxious to get to know Prince Igor before they were married and he could imagine nothing that would upset her more than if the Prince arrived just before the wedding ceremony.

She would then have no chance of first becoming friends as she wished to do.

The Earl's voice took on a distinctly sharp tone as he suggested to the Lord Chamberlain,

"I think you should send a messenger to Prince Igor immediately to say my niece has arrived and it is essential that he should be here to meet her as soon as possible."

"I will do so, my Lord, but I hope you will believe me when I tell you that I did, in my last letter, make it very clear that he should be here to meet Her Royal Highness and then spend time with her before the actual ceremony took place."

"I am sure you have done your very best, but I am thinking of my niece's feelings. She is extremely anxious to know her bridegroom before they are actually joined in Holy Matrimony."

"I can well understand and I will send a messenger on horseback to Prince Igor's Palace. But I cannot help thinking he must be on his way here after what I wrote to him earlier."

It was an apology and the Earl could only accept that it was not the Lord Chamberlain's fault.

At the same time he felt that it was extraordinarily offensive of Prince Igor not to be present.

He reflected yet again that it would be very difficult to persuade Tarena that she must marry a man she had not even met, if that was indeed still Prince Igor's intention.

Tarena had so many other things to think about that she had really forgotten about Prince Igor until she was changing for dinner.

She asked her new Karlovan lady's-maid if there was a big formal dinner party that evening.

The lady's-maid replied,

"Only those, Your Royal Highness, you arrived with and I think the Lord Chamberlain."

Then Tarena asked her,

"Surely Prince Igor of Dubnik is here in the Palace?"

"I don't think so, Your Royal Highness."

"Then find out for me," Tarena insisted as she sat down at the dressing table.

When she gazed at her face in the mirror, she could not help being aware that her eyes were shining and her lips were smiling.

She knew that the events of the afternoon had taken the Prime Minister and his Cabinet completely by surprise and yet according to Count Vladimir what had happened had been a great success.

She would respect his opinion rather than that of anyone else.

They had been so close on the Battleship and had spent so much time together.

She had sensed, although of course she had not said so, that he was anxious when they went down the gangway towards the platform on their arrival this morning.

She too was nervous that the speech he had written for her would not be a success.

But she had done things her own way.

As that had been unmistakably satisfactory, it was something which made her no longer feel frightened of being in Karlova.

Now she was feeling glad that she had come to take her father's place.

'I am sure Papa will help me,' she thought. 'The words seemed to come to my lips without having to think about them.'

She had been very conscious that the men waiting in stony silence were just the type of people, who might be persuaded by the Russian agents to rebel against those in authority and let the enemy take over the City.

Once they had done that, the Russians would gain possession of Karlova with virtually no resistance.

She had not asked the Count how large the Army of Karlova was, but she was almost certain that there were not as many trained men as there should be.

As she ruminated about her predicament, she then remembered once again that the Count's father believed he had found gold in the mountains.

She had read several books about those who had explored the world for rare minerals to satisfy the growing demands of the industrialised countries of Europe.

She was well aware that in many mountains such as the Caucasus, there was not only gold but a great many other minerals of great value.

'We will have to prospect in our mountains,' she thought. 'I wonder if Prince Igor will be interested in the discovery of saleable minerals, which could make Karlova rich and unafraid of the Russians.'

But it was too soon to bring up the subject yet.

However, it was at the back of her mind and again she had the feeling that her father was guiding her and telling her what she should do.

'How I wish I could remember him,' she mused. 'If only he could have brought Mama here to Karlova with him instead of having to marry that Princess Catrina of Dubnik, we could all have lived here in this lovely Palace and been very very happy.'

Even as she dreamed of this intriguing possibility, she was longing to explore the Palace closely and then she remembered that Prince Igor had not yet arrived.

Tomorrow she would hear of the plans that had been made for her Coronation in the Cathedral and later for her wedding.

'Perhaps something has happened to him and he will not turn up at all,' she told herself with a glimmer of hope in her heart.

The mere thought was intriguing, although it was against her better judgement even to dream that it had actually happened.

Then she told herself that if he had been injured in an accident, the Lord Chamberlain would surely have been advised at once.

He was in fact just showing her, by not being there to meet her, that to him she was of little or no significance.

Tarena enjoyed a deliciously hot bath and then put on one of the prettiest gowns she and her uncle had bought in Bond Street.

Then she walked slowly downstairs.

There was a woman she had not encountered before waiting beside the Lord Chamberlain in the hall.

He moved forward and announced with a flourish,

"May I present, Your Royal Highness, La Comtesse de Sâvairé who is to be your Lady-in-Waiting."

The woman dropped a deep curtsy and Tarena held out her hand.

"It is most kind of you, but I am afraid you will find me rather different from anyone else you have looked after."

"The Comtesse will help you to learn about what is expected in this country," the Lord Chamberlain explained, "and what has happened in the past."

Tarena smiled at him.

"What would be more helpful," she replied, "is if I can give you new ideas and continue to do the unexpected in the future."

She knew at once by the expression in the Lord Chamberlain's eyes that he was horrified that there should be *any* change.

She wanted to laugh.

Yet she walked sedately towards the room where they were to meet before dinner and the Comtesse followed her.

She was reasonably pretty, but as dinner progressed Tarena thought she would not be very much help to her. Certainly not with the changes she intended to make in the routine of the Palace or the City.

When dinner was over, an Officer appeared.

He had come to report to the Count that the people were letting off fireworks in the main Square of the City and he wondered if a detachment of soldiers should go down to make sure that there was no trouble.

"It's a good idea," the Count declared. "But I have a feeling that they are letting off fireworks simply because they are so pleased with all they have seen and heard about their new Queen. It's certainly not as dangerous as if there were pistol shots!"

The Officer smiled.

"I thought, sir, I should let you know what was happening."

"I am delighted to hear it. And if you do go to the Square, you might suggest that some decorations should be put up on the roads and flags flying from the windows."

Tarena gave an exclamation.

"Of course, that was what was missing! I never thought of it. Now I realise that there was not a flag to be seen when we drove up to the Palace. Nor were there any decorations on the houses or on the trees."

"I noticed it too," said the Count. "I have been told that while I have been away Russian agents have infiltrated into the City and have tried to persuade the people that they would suffer under another King and Queen and would be far happier if they were under Russian rule."

Tarena gave a little cry of horror.

"Has that already been happening?" she asked. "I believed that when my father was alive there was very little subversion and the Russians had left Karlova alone."

"They have most certainly worked very quickly and quietly, but there is no doubt they have been infiltrating in their usual underhand way into the poorer parts of the City and among the unemployed and disaffected."

Tarena was listening intently as the Count went on,

"I am told they paint a picture of how rich everyone will be if they prefer Russian rule to that of the Royalty of past years."

"What can be done about it?" Tarena asked the Count nervously.

"You have made exactly the right beginning. The Russians must have felt very frustrated when they heard what occurred this afternoon at the Port."

"You really think it will make a difference?"

"A very great difference," he replied. "You have started off on the right foot. What you really have to do now is to forge ahead in your own inimitable way without any interference from any of us."

"That sounds exactly what I want," Tarena agreed. "But I cannot do it without your help, Count Vladimir."

"And you know you only have to ask," the Count said in a low voice.

Tarena smiled at him.

Then she was aware of the Comtesse watching her from across the table.

Quite suddenly she knew the woman was hostile.

She did not know why she felt this way.

She could only sense it, just as she had often felt vibrations emanating from her uncle's acquaintances.

She had known instantly when, although some were flattering him, they really had no regard for him.

'There is something about her,' she told herself. 'When I am alone with the Count, I must ask him who appointed the Comtesse and why she was chosen.'

"You are very silent, Tarena," her uncle said to her unexpectedly. "Are you feeling tired?"

"I am both tired and relaxed, so I hope no one will think it rude of me if I retire fairly early. We will have a long day tomorrow."

"I am only too willing to agree with you," the Earl responded.

"Of course you must," the Comtesse came in, "and, if you are wise, you will rest tomorrow and not go into the City or bother with the people who will doubtless come knocking at the door after you have encouraged them in a way that has never happened before."

Tarena was silent for a moment and then she turned to the Lord Chamberlain,

"Will you please make it absolutely clear that if anyone wants to meet me I will see them immediately?"

He hesitated before acknowledging the instruction and Tarena continued,

"I think it is very important now I have arrived to let the people know that I am available to them to listen to all their troubles and sorrows.

"And of course to try to make things better for the poorer people, who I understand do not have good schools, nor is there a hospital available for them."

"Oh, there is a hospital of some sort," the Lord Chamberlain bumbled. "But it's not in the City."

"I was told it is ten miles away. If you have a sick child, you can hardly carry it ten miles before it receives the attention it needs."

The Lord Chamberlain stared at her.

"Is Your Royal Highness really telling us that we need to build a hospital here in the Capital?"

"If you don't have one at the moment, I think it's extraordinary that you have not realised before that there must be a hospital nearby for people to go to when they or their children are ill."

She was fully aware as she was speaking that the Lord Chamberlain was again absolutely astonished.

It was quite obvious he had thought that she was only a young girl and it would be left to her husband to make changes if there were to be any at all.

He certainly did not expect that the moment Tarena arrived that she would be thinking about improvements.

"You will have to talk to the Prime Minister," he said. "But I think you will find, Your Royal Highness, that such ideas, which I know are put forward in all countries, are usually just a flash in the pan and fade away when the cost is reckoned and there is no money to meet them."

"Are you telling me in a polite way that Karlova is bankrupt?" Tarena asked only slightly aggressively.

The Lord Chamberlain could not have been more surprised if she had shouted at him.

"No, no, of course not. I did not mean anything of the sort. I merely implied that the populace, or rather the poorer people in the City, are never satisfied with anything they receive. They always want more. We first have to concentrate on the celebrations of Your Royal Highness's wedding and Coronation and forget those who are never happy however much you pander to them."

It was quite a speech and everyone at the table was listening to it.

Then Tarena countered quietly,

"I understand, my Lord, what you are saying. And naturally I am completely and absolutely convinced that every great City should boast a modern hospital."

CHAPTER FIVE

The next morning Tarena woke early and thought over everything that had happened the day before.

She was happier because in some ways it had all gone far better than she had anticipated.

Equally she was intelligent enough to realise that an enormous number of difficulties still lay ahead.

She had taken breakfast in the boudoir next door.

Then she was informed that the Count would like to see her.

She had dressed before breakfast and had quickly arranged her hair just in case it had become untidy whilst she was eating.

Then she called out for the Count to come in.

He was smiling as he walked towards her.

"I might have known," he sighed, "that you would be up and ready, because we have a great deal to do."

"I am aware of that, Count Vladimir. What do we do first?"

"I think that first of all you should pay a visit to the Cathedral where you are to be married in the morning of the day after tomorrow."

Tarena gave a little exclamation.

"How can I possibly be married as quickly as that when I have not yet met Prince Igor?"

There was silence for a moment before the Count replied,

"I think it is best to be frank and tell you that the Prince is apparently somewhat reluctant to marry you, but a marriage *must* take place."

"Why so quickly?"

The Count walked towards the window so that he had his back to her.

She knew without his saying anything that he was debating with himself whether he should tell her the truth or not.

"I suppose," she said in a small voice, "the Russian situation is now worse than you expected."

The Count turned round.

"You are right, of course you are right. You are too astute for me to lie to you, Your Royal Highness."

"I would be very disappointed if you did," Tarena flashed back at him. "I have felt that I can trust you and we were always frank with each other when we were on *The Royal Sovereign*."

The Count smiled and Tarena indicated to him to sit down opposite her.

"What I have learnt since I came back," he began, "is that things are even more serious than I imagined."

Tarena did not say anything.

She was looking at him wide-eyed and listening to everything he was saying.

"The trouble is," the Count continued, "after your father died they were rather slow in asking for help from England. The Russians, thinking it was impossible for the Queen to find anyone to send, were encouraged to believe they could take over Karlova swiftly without any serious opposition."

"I suppose that means," Tarena replied after a little pause, "that there are not as many soldiers as we need and the Russian troops are more formidable than we thought."

The Count gave a little laugh.

"You are so intelligent," he said, "that sometimes you frighten me. I feel that you know more than I do and certainly a great deal more than the General whose job it is to defend Karlova."

"Tell me exactly what has happened," she begged.

"When I left here to come to England, it was not too bad. We knew that the dreadful Russians were stirring up trouble wherever they could and bribing in one way or another those who were out of work or critical of the way their country was ruled."

"I have read that is what they have been doing in other parts of the Balkans and I know how successful they have been in certain other countries."

"They have started to use the very same underhand methods here and unfortunately they have been to some extent successful."

Tarena gave a deep sigh.

"Oh, what can we do about it?" she implored him.

The Count rose to his feet almost as if he found it impossible to keep still in a comfortable chair.

"The strongest and most effective weapon we have at the moment," he asserted, "is still *you*!"

Tarena looked at him.

"Are you just flattering me or telling me the truth?"

"I am telling the truth and I most certainly would not lie at this critical moment. The way you managed your arrival yesterday was not only brilliant on your part but a major blow the Russians did not anticipate."

"Then what are they doing about it?"

"What they are doing now," the Count answered, "is bringing up more troops. A great number had already been positioned to threaten us whilst I was away."

Tarena gave a little cry.

"So we are overpowered!" she exclaimed.

"All except for you," the Count replied.

For a moment there was silence and then Tarena spread out her hands.

"Tell me what I can do, Count Vladimir."

He smiled at her.

"I thought you would understand. I am going to take you now right into the heart of the City, ostensibly to inspect the Cathedral. But I am confident that something will happen, as it did yesterday, that will make the people realise, as I have for a long time, just how wonderful you really are."

He spoke in a way that was somehow very moving and Tarena looked up at him.

As their eyes met, it was difficult to look away.

"You *are* wonderful," the Count said very quietly. "So wonderful that there are no words for me to tell you what you mean to – Karlova."

Tarena knew at once that he had been about to say, "*to me,*" then changed it at the last moment.

She felt a little shy and there was a sharp feeling in her breast she had never known before.

She rose to her feet.

"I will fetch my hat," she suggested, "and then – I will be ready to go wherever you wish to take me."

She did not look at the Count as she went towards her bedroom.

But she felt that his eyes were following her.

She sensed that there was an expression in them that she did not dare put into words even to herself.

When they walked downstairs, she found that the Comtesse de Sâvairé was waiting for her with one of the Palace equerries.

She had hoped that she would be able to go alone with the Count, but she recognised that in her new position it would be impossible and so she had to have attendants waiting on her.

She also found when they went outside that there was an escort of six soldiers on horseback and they would ride on either side of her open carriage.

"I suppose all this is necessary," she said in a low voice to the Count.

He understood exactly what she was asking.

"You are already the Queen of this country, Your Royal Highness."

Tarena gave a little laugh.

"It is something I find very hard to remember!"

The Count smiled.

She stepped into the carriage, aware as she did so that the Lord Chamberlain had come hurrying into the hall behind them.

He was looking irritated as if he felt he should have been asked for his permission for the Queen to go into the City.

But it was too late for him to do anything.

As the carriage moved off, Tarena bent forward to raise her hand to him.

"I rather think he wanted to take you into the City himself," the Count piped up. "That is why I suggested we leave so early and so quickly."

The equerry sitting opposite them laughed.

"It is always the same with you, Vladimir," he said. "You always strike first, and ask permission to do so when it is too late to stop you!"

"If that is my reputation, Ernest. I am not going to argue about it. But I do find listening to people wondering whether one should or should not do something is a terrible waste of time."

They all laughed at this, except, Tarena noticed, the Comtesse.

She had curtsied low to her when she appeared, but again Tarena had the impression, as she had last night, that the Comtesse was somehow hostile.

She wondered why, but thought it a mistake to ask too many questions at this stage.

Therefore she sat back in the seat and tried to take in as much as she could of the City as they passed along the road.

She was, however, fully aware that the Count was looking from side to side as the horses drove them forward.

There was a pistol in his belt and the soldiers riding on either side of the carriage were heavily armed.

As they progressed further into the City, she saw that the buildings were now not so tall nor as substantial as those nearer to the Palace.

In fact as they drew into what she thought must be the centre of the City, the houses were in urgent need of repair and a number of what looked like factories were not working.

She could see the tall spires of the Cathedral long before they reached the Square in the City centre.

When they arrived, she was astonished to see that the Square was filled with people.

They were not looking towards the Cathedral, but towards the other side where there was a statue of one of the former Kings of Karlova.

Sitting below it, yet raised above ground level, was a man wearing what seemed to be a Judge's wig.

She was then aware that the Count was staring at the crowd.

Finally he spoke up,

"I had no idea that this would be happening here today."

"What is it?" Tarena asked apprehensively.

"Something I don't want you to see," he answered sharply. "I think it would be best if we turned back now and came back this afternoon."

"I don't understand. What is happening?"

Before the Count could reply, the equerry cried,

"I know what it is! A man is being punished for stealing by having his hand cut off."

"I was not told that this was happening," the Count said angrily, "and I have no wish for Her Royal Highness to be involved in this sort of spectacle. We must turn round and go back."

But this would not be easy.

By this time the horses were moving very slowly as the crowd was so thick and it was obvious that it would be impossible for them to turn round without a great deal of manoeuvring.

It was then that Tarena, looking towards the statue and the Judge sitting below it, demanded firmly,

"Stop the carriage!"

The equerry stared at her.

"But Your Royal Highness – " he began.

"Stop the carriage!" Tarena insisted. "I intend to speak to the man and ask him why he is being punished."

"I think that would be a great mistake," the Count advised quickly.

"If I am the Queen," Tarena answered, "you have to obey me. I wish the carriage to stop now and I intend to get out."

For a moment she thought the Count was about to defy her.

Instead, as if he felt that it was something he was obliged to do, he said,

"Of course, Your Royal Highness's orders must be obeyed."

The Equerry ordered the coachman to draw in the horses and halt.

As the footman sprang down to open the carriage door, Tarena climbed out, followed by the Count and the equerry.

The large throng moved rapidly out of her way.

They stared at her in surprise as she walked through the crowd towards the statue.

It took Tarena a little time, but the people fell back as she approached.

While she thought that some of them smiled, the rest looked at her as they had yesterday, in what she felt was a somewhat hostile manner.

She reached the statue.

The Judge was sitting on a platform that was raised high enough for him to be seen by everyone in the Square.

Below him there was a man in handcuffs held by two large men who were obviously Policemen.

Facing them behind a heavy block of wood stood another man holding a sharp-edged axe in his hand.

As Tarena stood in front of the Judge, she looked up at him and said, speaking slowly and distinctively,

"I have come, Your Honour, to enquire, as Queen of Karlova, what judgement is being passed by you on this man who I can see is your prisoner?"

The Judge, who had been somewhat bewildered at her appearance and had not been aware that she was the Queen, rose and made a low bow.

"I am greatly honoured that Your Royal Highness should be interested in my duty today, which is to punish a low criminal."

"Please be seated, Your Honour, and tell me what this man has done."

The Judge seated himself and, putting his hands up to see that his wig was in the correct position, he replied,

"He has stolen, Your Royal Highness, and stealing is forbidden by law. If a man disobeys the law, then he has, if he is found guilty, to surrender one of his hands."

Tarena glanced at the man with the axe.

She realised that it was sharp and shining and the block of wood had clearly been in use for many years – the blood of unfortunate criminals had left their mark on it.

"May I ask, Your Honour, what this man has stolen which will meet with such a terrible punishment."

It was then, before the Judge could reply to her, that the prisoner who had been staring intently at Tarena in sheer astonishment, cried out,

"It were food, Your Majesty. Food for me children who be dying of starvation till they could hardly cry, they be so weak."

As he finished speaking, Tarena looked up at the Judge.

96

"Is this true, Your Honour?" she enquired.

Before the Judge could reply, there was a scream from the crowd.

A woman in rags appeared, bringing with her three small children.

She flung herself on the ground in front of Tarena and sobbed,

"It be the whole truth, Your Majesty. The children here be starving as you can see for yourself. We has had nothing to eat for weeks except what we can find in the woods. He be a good father and when they cries he says he couldn't take it no more and went out to steal a chicken."

There was no doubt that the woman was telling the truth and Tarena had only to look at the children to see that they were painfully thin and emaciated.

As if the Judge thought matters were going too far, he declared,

"This man has committed a crime. And now, if Your Royal Highness will permit, we will go ahead and make him pay for it by losing his left hand."

As the Judge was speaking loudly and clearly, there was not a murmur from the crowd.

As the two Policemen holding the prisoner, led him towards the block, Tarena held up her hand.

"No!" she cried out. "No! As long as I am Queen in Karlova, taking my father's place and bringing to you, I hope, peace and happiness, no man shall suffer because he has quite naturally tried to save his children from dying. In fact I think that the removal of a man's hand is a cruel punishment which is long out of date."

For a moment, as she had spoken clearly, there was complete silence.

Then, as the crowd round her realised what she had said, they began to cheer.

It was the Judge who seemed to recover first.

"If that is Your Royal Highness's order," he said, "I can only obey it. I then presume, as the prisoner is not to be punished for his crime, that he be allowed to go free."

"I wish to ask him a question first," Tarena held up her hand.

The two Policemen, who were about to release the prisoner, kept a tight hold of him as she came nearer.

"Tell me," she asked, "why you did not find work so that you could afford to buy food for your children?"

"Although I've tried and tried, there be no work for gardeners in the City," he answered. "People who can afford it have left for the country. Although I've asked at many houses no one wants to pay a gardener right now."

Tarena guessed that the richer people in the City knew what the Russians were intending.

They had therefore moved out as soon as possible so that when the fighting and bloodshed began they would not be involved.

"So you are a gardener," she said. "Well I am quite certain a gardener can always be used at the Palace. If you will go there immediately, I will see that you are employed and that your children have enough food so they will no longer be hungry."

"I'll serve Your Majesty till I die," the man cried.

Even as he spoke, Tarena turned round to face the crowd behind her.

"These children are starving," she stated, raising her voice. "It is something that must never happen again to children in this City over which I reign. Is there anyone here now who will give them something to eat so they will look a little happier than they do now?"

There was a movement in the crowd.

Then, as the Count beckoned over a man selling sweets and fruit, they once again began to cheer.

As he joined them, Tarena took from his tray with her own hands something that looked to her like buns and handed them to the children.

The mother, who was still kneeling on the ground, kissed the hem of Tarena's dress, murmuring as she did so that her prayers had been answered.

She was saying that God had sent Her Majesty like 'an Angel from Heaven to save them.'

As the children grabbed the buns and stuffed them into their mouths, Tarena turned round and declared,

"I blame no one for this, but as long as I am here in Karlova it must not happen again. No child must ever go hungry and no one must again suffer this out-of-date and barbarous punishment."

She paused and looked round at the crowd before she added,

"A professional thief must be sent to prison in the normal way. I only beg of you all to see that in the future my wishes are carried out and no child suffers as these poor mites have suffered."

The crowd was quiet while she spoke and then the cheers seemed to be carried up into the sky.

The men were waving their hats and the women their handkerchiefs.

When Tarena looked round, she saw that the Judge had very wisely withdrawn and his chair was now empty.

As the crowd came nearer, she moved a little closer to the Count as if she was afraid of being crushed by them.

"Now we must leave," he suggested. "If you will walk to the Cathedral, Your Royal Highness, it is what the people will expect you to do."

The Count was smiling as he spoke.

She knew that, although she had done something unexpected once again, he was not annoyed with her.

The equerry walked ahead to try to clear the way.

As she followed, the women went down on their knees to kiss the hem of her gown as the mother of the children had done.

The Count paid the seller of the sweets handsomely and he was looking pleased.

It took them some time to reach the Cathedral.

When they did so, it was to find the Archbishop and several of the Clergy standing on the steps ready to greet them.

Apparently they had wondered what was happening when they heard the crowd cheering and they had been told by the onlookers what had occurred.

As Tarena walked up the steps of the Cathedral, the crowd was still cheering.

A great number of them had followed her and she turned round and waved her hand.

They roared out their applause while waving their handkerchiefs and anything else they could find.

Tarena could see the children were still clustered round the man with the food, eating everything they were given with their mother still crying beside them and their father had his arm round her shoulders.

There was far too much noise for Tarena to say anything, so she could only wave.

When she disappeared into the Cathedral, followed by the Archbishop, they could still hear the cheers, even when the doors of the Cathedral were closed behind them.

"Is it really true, Your Royal Highness," enquired the Archbishop, "that you have said that the traditional punishment for stealing, which has been in force in this country for at least five hundred years, is no longer to be carried out?"

"It is out of date and barbaric," replied Tarena. "I am only totally surprised that Your Grace did not have it abolished a long time ago."

The Archbishop looked embarrassed.

And then Count Vladimir proposed,

"We have come, Your Grace, to talk about the wedding that is to take place on the day after tomorrow."

"Yes, yes of course," the Archbishop responded.

Tarena knew he was feeling guilty about what had just occurred.

He showed her round the Cathedral, which was very impressive.

He then explained the wedding ceremony in detail.

The Marriage Service was to be followed by the Coronation, she and Prince Igor being crowned as King and Queen of Karlova.

"You don't think," Tarena said a little hesitantly, "that it would be a good idea to wait until at least the end of the week?"

She was thinking as she spoke that she had not yet met Prince Igor.

The Archbishop looked at the crowd and shook his head.

"I have been told, Your Royal Highness," he said in an apologetic tone, "that the situation is very dangerous in the City. We are hoping and praying that we will be able to prevent the Russians from overthrowing the throne."

Tarena felt there was nothing more she could say.

At the same time she felt it was quite wrong and unnatural that she should be made to marry a man she had not yet met.

As if the Count realised what she was feeling, he began to ask questions about the ceremony itself and the Archbishop was only too willing to supply answers.

Finally, when she had seen everything including the two crowns waiting for her and Prince Igor, Tarena turned to the Count,

"I think we should return to the Palace."

"That is what I was thinking too," he replied. "But Your Royal Highness will be aware that there may be a large crowd waiting to tell you what you mean to them."

"I only hope that's true," remarked Tarena.

The Archbishop accompanied them as they walked down the aisle towards the door and, as they reached it, he said,

"I do promise you, Your Royal Highness, that the Service will not be too long or too exhausting. Equally we must ask for the very special blessing of God and that you will be permitted to preserve the peace that your beloved father brought to our people."

"That is just what I intend to do, but I realise that things are much more difficult now, and I know it is only by the grace of God Himself that Karlova can remain free."

The Archbishop smiled at her.

Then, as the doors were opened, they looked out to see that the large crowd was still there.

As Tarena came out into the Square, women and children ran forward to throw flower petals in front of her.

There were not very many of them, but she found it very touching to walk on wild flowers and leaves that had obviously been hastily picked.

The crowd started cheering as she appeared and by the time she reached the bottom of the steps the sound was like the roar of the sea.

As she climbed into the carriage, the people threw more wild flowers into it.

The horses could only move very slowly through the throng and, as they did so, the women shouted,

"God Bless Your Majesty, and we'll not lose you! You can be sure of that."

It was all very moving.

Only when they were out of the inner City and travelling down the roads with trees on both sides, was Tarena able to put down her arm and stop waving.

"You are wonderful! Completely wonderful!" the Count sighed.

"I have never seen anything like it!" the equerry exclaimed. "No one in the City will ever forget this day."

Only the Comtesse said nothing and looking at her, Tarena realised that she was almost sneering at what had occurred.

As the horses moved more quickly, Tarena said,

"I have the feeling, Comtesse, that you do not agree with me that such an ancient but cruel punishment should be abolished."

"I think those sort of people don't respect any other form of punishment," the Comtesse answered her sharply. "You will soon find out that there will be more thieving in Karlova than there has ever been before."

Tarena felt that this was plain speaking and almost a challenge to her personally, but felt it best not to reply.

She made up her mind that once she was crowned Queen that she would choose her own Ladies-in-Waiting and the Comtesse would not be amongst them.

As if the Count sensed her thoughts, he remarked,

"I had no idea that there would be a Judgement, as they always call it, in the Square this morning. I can only apologise that you had to be involved in anything quite so unpleasant."

"I think it was the best thing that could possibly have happened. I will make sure that such cruelty is not inflicted in future. What is more, as I said to the people, no child in the country I rule over will be allowed to suffer from starvation."

"You are so right. It is a disgrace that should not be allowed and would not have persisted if it had not been for fear of the Russians."

"I thought from what that man said that all the richer citizens, who could leave, have already gone."

"He is right," the Count replied. "They began to be frightened immediately your father died and they have been moving as quickly as they could to the other side of the country, while some have actually gone further still."

"Do you think they will come back, Count?"

"I think that once you are Queen they will all want to return to their homeland."

The equerry said the same.

Yet as Tarena looked at the Comtesse, there was no doubt that there was a cynical twist to her red lips – and a look that proclaimed only too clearly she thought that the people who had run away would stay away.

'I dislike her! I positively dislike her!' Tarena said to herself.

Yet she knew it would be difficult to do anything before she was actually crowned.

At the same time it was exciting to know that she was being treated as the Queen already.

She was quite certain that the barbaric punishment for thieving would not be inflicted again so long as she was the Queen of Karlova.

They returned to the Palace where fortunately they had not yet learnt of what had occurred in the City.

The Lord Chamberlain busied himself explaining to Tarena that she was to receive a deputation of the wives of the Cabinet during the afternoon.

"Just the wives?" she enquired.

The Lord Chamberlain smiled.

"I am afraid so. The Prime Minister has called a special meeting for this afternoon and tomorrow we are to discuss the final arrangements for the wedding."

He glanced at Count Vladimir as he spoke.

Tarena sensed, without their saying it in words, that they were scared the Russians would, at the last moment, somehow prevent her wedding and Coronation from taking place.

It was one thing, she thought, to have made at least some of the people pleased and respectful to her.

But there were still Russians who had penetrated into the City and had then acquired a significant following amongst the opponents of the present regime.

And their armed forces were outside waiting for the opportunity to take over.

Almost as if instinctively she was looking to him for help, Tarena turned to the Count and he said quietly so that only she could hear,

"You have taken the first two fences in style. Do not be afraid of the next ones."

Tarena smiled apprehensively.

"Do you really believe, Count Vladimir, that we can reach the winning post?"

"You are halfway there already and I am betting every penny I possess on you."

105

Tarena laughed out loud and it seemed somehow to break the tension.

"Luncheon will be served in a few minutes time," the Lord Chamberlain announced.

"I would like to tidy myself first."

As Tarena turned, the Lord Chamberlain added,

"I think I should inform Your Royal Highness that Prince Igor has just arrived and will be meeting you before luncheon, if you wish it, in the private rooms where His Majesty, your father, always received special guests."

For a moment Tarena felt as though her heart had stopped beating.

"Thank you, my Lord, that is an excellent idea."

Then, as if she was running away from something that terrified her, she hurried up the stairs, wondering what the Count would think of Prince Igor's belated appearance.

When she reached her own room, her lady's-maid was waiting to help her take off her hat and tidy her hair and to pour out the water to wash her hands.

"Did everything go well, Your Royal Highness?" she asked. "And did you like the Cathedral?"

"I liked it very much," Tarena replied vaguely.

She was glad that no one for the moment at the Palace knew what had happened during the morning.

Because the bottom of her dress had been touched by so many hands she changed into one of the other gowns she had bought in London.

When finally she was dressed, she walked slowly down the stairs.

As expected, the Lord Chamberlain was waiting for her and Tarena forced herself to smile at him.

"I am sorry if I kept you, my Lord."

"It's all right, Your Royal Highness," he answered. "I have told them to serve luncheon a quarter-of-an-hour late."

It was with difficulty that Tarena prevented herself from saying that perhaps fifteen minutes would be too long for her to be alone with Prince Igor.

But she recognised that she must behave with the propriety expected of her.

She walked slowly behind the Lord Chamberlain until they were in a part of the Palace she had been told her father kept entirely for himself.

She had not been surprised to learn that one of the rooms contained a magnificent library.

The room they were now approaching looked out over the garden at the back of the Palace where there was a profusion of flowers that her father had loved so much.

The Lord Chamberlain opened the door and then announced in a stentorian tone,

"Her Royal Highness, Princess Tarena."

There was a man standing by the window.

As Tarena entered, she realised he had deliberately not turned round, but remained steadily looking out with his back to her.

He was tall and she saw that his hair was dark.

As he turned round and she walked towards him, she knew with what her father had often called her *Third Eye* that there was something wrong with him and she did not like him.

When she drew nearer and she forced herself not to hurry, she saw that he was fairly good-looking.

But there was definitely a vibration coming from him that told her with the instinct that had never failed her there was something very negative about him.

She put out her hand.

He bent over it in the French style and his lips did not actually touch her skin.

"It is indeed a great pleasure to meet Your Royal Highness," he began. "I do hope that we will be able to bring peace and prosperity to Karlova."

Even as he spoke, Tarena knew that the words had been chosen for him and he did not believe in them.

She did not know why she was so positive, but she knew, without his saying another word, that he was quite certain that they could never bring peace and prosperity to Karlova together.

Yet if that was so, why was he here?

He asked politely what sort of voyage she had had on the way from England and he was interested in the fact that she had travelled in one of the new British Battleships. He added as to how much he enjoyed a sea voyage himself.

It was all very polite, but a purely conventional conversation.

Tarena felt they were fencing with sharp weapons.

She was sure, although he made no sign of it, that he disliked her as much as she disliked him.

Their conversation was so artificial and so obvious that she almost felt like laughing out loud as they were behaving exactly as was expected of them.

Neither of them was being in the least sincere.

It was an utter relief when the Lord Chamberlain opened the door,

"Luncheon is served, Your Royal Highness."

"We must not keep the chef waiting," Tarena said.

She walked towards the door knowing that Prince Igor was following her.

She was wondering, as she did so, how she could possibly escape from him.

'I cannot marry him, I cannot,' she thought as they walked to the dining room where she saw that a number of guests were waiting for them.

The Prime Minister had obviously been informed of Prince Igor's late arrival.

He was there waiting with his Minister for Foreign Affairs and three or four other Members of the Cabinet.

As they entered the room and their guests bowed, Tarena noticed that the only other woman beside herself at luncheon was her Lady-in-Waiting, the Comtesse.

She knew that, if they had invited the wife of the Prime Minister, it would have meant the other wives also would have expected to be present.

They had therefore made it a small luncheon party.

The Lord Chamberlain was introducing Prince Igor to everyone present, beginning with the Earl and ending eventually with the Comtesse.

"I think perhaps, Prince Igor," he said, "you may have met the Comtesse de Sâvairé before. She has most kindly consented to become Lady-in-Waiting to Her Royal Highness."

The Comtesse curtsied and held out her hand.

Prince Igor took it in his and to Tarena's surprise actually kissed it.

Then, as she moved towards the top of the table, where their chairs had been placed tactfully side by side, she was convinced, as she saw the expression on his face, that she disliked him even more than when she had first seen him.

She had no idea what was wrong.

Yet every instinct within her told her that he was not what he pretended to be, and was in fact, although it seemed ridiculous, an underhand and wicked man.

CHAPTER SIX

Tarena woke early and jumped out of bed.

Last night she had endured an appallingly boring evening.

So she had whispered to Count Vladimir when she had bade everyone goodnight,

"Can I ride with you tomorrow morning?"

She had mentioned the idea to him once before and, now without prevaricating, he replied,

"I will be ready at seven o'clock."

She smiled at him and slipped up the stairs before anyone could stop her.

She was running away from Prince Igor, who she thought had been more unpleasant at dinner than earlier.

He had talked on, laying down the law, about the current political situation in Africa in which no one was particularly interested.

He managed to maintain this flow of conversation with the Prime Minister, but had ignored Tarena and did not speak to her at all during dinner. And he had treated the Count as if he was too insignificant to pass the time of day with.

The Minister for Foreign Affairs was a little old and deaf and had therefore not attempted to interrupt.

'If I have to sit through many more dinner parties like this one,' Terena reflected, 'I will go mad!'

After dinner was over Prince Igor looked at some of the paintings in the picture gallery and the reception rooms and made supercilious remarks about them as if he had an expert knowledge of artists.

Terena might have been more interested if she had not thought he was doing this to avoid having to talk to her.

When they finally returned to the drawing room, where coffee and liqueurs were being served, Prince Igor, quite obviously, seated himself with a man on each side of him – and ignored the women completely.

'If that is how he is going to treat me in the future,' Terena thought, 'I could not stand it.'

It was not only his behaviour she disliked but the man himself.

But she recognised that for the sake of the country she had to make the best of it.

With a tremendous effort, after the Prime Minister had left and the Minister for Foreign Affairs was talking to the Count, Tarena suggested to Prince Igor,

"I think Your Royal Highness that we should get together and talk about our future."

He stared at her.

She had the feeling that he was about to ask why and then he replied,

"I think that anything we have to discuss can wait until after the wedding."

"On the contrary," Tarena countered, "I have a good number of questions I would like to ask you before I actually become your wife. I assure you it is usual to know someone well before one is forced, as we are being, into marriage on such a brief acquaintance."

Prince Igor shrugged his shoulders.

"The only matters we should discuss are the affairs of the country and they I would suggest are best left until I have learnt from those in authority the exact position here in Karlova."

She thought that he was being obviously obtuse.

Moreover, he was not even looking at her while she spoke to him, which she thought intolerably rude.

"Shall we meet in the garden after breakfast?" she nevertheless forced herself to ask. "It is very beautiful and I don't think you have yet seen it."

"I will think about it," he replied, "and will send an equerry to let you know my plans. But I anticipate that tomorrow I will be rather busy with the Prime Minister and other Members of the Cabinet."

It was not just what he said, but the way he said it that made Tarena angry.

She felt that he was dismissing her as someone of no consequence whatsoever.

If that was how he intended to behave in their married life, she could see that he would make things even more difficult for her than she had feared.

However, she had learnt many years ago to control her temper, so she responded in quite a pleasant voice,

"I think one of the first things we should do is to look into the jurisdiction of the country. I was shocked today to find that a man was about to have his hand cut off because he had stolen food for his starving children."

"I expect he deserved what was coming to him," Prince Igor grunted. "I am sure you realise that a woman interfering in the public affairs in any country is usually considered a tiresome nuisance."

For a moment Tarena was simply taken aback by his reply.

Then she felt her anger rising.

Almost, as if he sensed it, the Count came to her side to say,

"I am sure that Your Royal Highness must be tired after such a long day when so much has happened. Try to get to sleep and then forget everything until it is daylight tomorrow."

Because she realised that he was being kind and considerate to her, she felt her heart moving towards him.

For a split second she forgot everything else, even Prince Igor standing sourly at her side.

Knowing that Count Vladimir was there, she was no longer angry but happy.

Without saying another word, Prince Igor walked out of the room.

There was no sign of the Comtesse who must have already left.

It was then that Tarena felt as if she was sending a cry for help to the Count from her heart.

She ran upstairs hoping the night would go quickly and, if she could ride tomorrow, she would at least forget Prince Igor for a while and her dislike of him.

Without bothering to send for her lady's-maid, she undressed herself and she had told the woman to put out her riding clothes before she went down to dinner.

She climbed gratefully into her comfortable bed.

*

The next morning it only took her a short time to slip into her riding habit.

When she left her room, she found that the Count was waiting for her in the corridor.

"Oh, you are here!" she called out excitedly.

"I thought as we are playing truant that we had better go out by a side door where we will not be seen by the servants and where the horses are waiting for us."

The Count then led the way down the corridor to a staircase Tarena had not noticed and when they went down it, she found there was a door that opened directly onto the garden where there were no sentries.

The Count did not speak, but led the way down a winding path.

A little below them, there were two lively-looking stallions being held by a groom.

The Count, without saying a word, lifted Tarena onto the side saddle of the horse she was to ride and then mounted himself on the other one, saying to the groom,

"Be waiting here in an hour when we will return."

The groom touched his forelock and they rode off with the Count leading the way.

He took her through the trees at the back of the Palace into a field that led to open land behind the City.

When they reached it, Tarena knew instinctively what he intended to do.

She pressed her stallion forward into a gallop and the Count did the same and then they were riding over long grass and butterflies and birds rose up in front of them.

It was some time before the Count pulled in his horse.

When Tarena looked round, she found they were quite a long way from the City. In fact she could only just see the roof of the Palace and little else.

"That was lovely!" she breathed.

"I thought it was a diversion you really needed," said the Count.

Now their two stallions were walking quietly side by side and then suddenly Tarena exploded,

"He is *horrible*! He is *beastly*! I cannot marry him!"

The words seemed to burst through her lips and for a moment she broke the beauty and the quiet around them.

"I knew you felt like that last night, but there is nothing we can do about it," the Count sighed.

"But we must! *We must!* How can I possibly be married to a man like that who intends to ignore me and to prevent me from taking any part in ruling the country – *my* country."

"He most certainly will not be able to do so. At the same time I do admit he is exceedingly unpleasant."

"I hate him! I hate him!" Tarena expostulated.

"Do you think I have not thought about that?" the Count said in a low voice. "Oh, my darling, if it was at all possible, I would save you."

For a moment Tarena could hardly believe her ears.

Then, as she looked at him questioningly, he added,

"I love you, of course I love you. I have loved you since the first moment I saw you and thought you were the most beautiful and perfect woman I had ever seen."

There was silence.

Then Tarena said in a voice he could hardly hear,

"I think – I love you – *too*."

"This is something you must not do," the Count insisted firmly. "It will only make you unhappy. I swear I will try to be man enough to bear it. But I could not live if I thought you were suffering too."

"I have never been – in love," Tarena admitted. "But I know now that I do love you. When you appear, I feel happy as if the sunshine envelopes me, but when you are not there – I am frightened and uncertain."

The Count closed his eyes as if it was agony to listen to her and then he said,

"You are clever enough and wonderful enough to know that the only person who could save this country is you."

"But do you imagine Prince Igor will let me do it?"

"I think once you are married he could be forced by the Cabinet to do what you want and to stop treating you as a woman of no stature."

"That is what he was deliberately doing last night. How can I help the people, as you and everybody else want me to do, if that is his attitude?"

"You will have to assert yourself as Queen," the Count said, "and you will have full support from the Prime Minister, the Cabinet and me."

"You are the only person who matters," Tarena answered. "But how, feeling as I do about you, can I live with a man like Prince Igor?"

The Count did not answer her, but she could see by the expression on his face the agony he was suffering.

"Oh, Vladimir," she exclaimed, calling him by his Christian name for the first time, "why don't we run away together?"

The Count turned to look at her and she could see the pain in his eyes.

"Do you suppose I have not thought of that?" he asked. "Night after night I have lain awake loving you and wanting you, but knowing full well that you were as far out of my reach as the furthest star in the firmament."

"Then why do – we not do what we really want – to do?" Tarena asked hesitatingly.

"Because we both know that without you Karlova is doomed. I don't want to frighten you, but you are the only hope we have at present of preventing the Russians from taking over."

The Count gave a deep sigh before he went on,

"They thought it was going to be easy, and so it would have been if you had been an ordinary, rather stupid Englishwoman. Instead it is you, beautiful Tarena, who has awakened your people, and now they are as excited about the wedding which will take place tomorrow as if they were children at a Christmas party."

"You really think they want me as their Queen?"

"They want you, oh, how they want you and I am told the Russians are absolutely furious that you have upset everything just as they had it so carefully planned."

"I want to be with you, Vladimir. I am frightened, very frightened of Prince Igor."

"I swear to you that I will help you and, although it will be an agony I cannot express, *I will dedicate my entire life to serving you and protecting you.*"

The Count spoke almost violently.

But Tarena asked him plaintively,

"Oh, Vladimir how can we be together, yet apart?"

He knew exactly what she meant.

"From this moment on, I will not tell you again how much I love you. But I will be there close to you, to help you if I can in the ruling of the country. We must, however, also control ourselves, knowing that without us the people will be at the mercy of the vile Russians."

"Why! Why did this have to happen to us?" Tarena asked. "I always hoped I would fall in love and be happy wherever I was with the man I loved and how could I have guessed, how could I have imagined for a moment when I came out here that I would find you?"

"I think perhaps we were meant to find each other," the Count said. "We can only pray that one day by some unbelievable miracle I can love you as it was meant when we were born."

"What you are saying, Vladimir, is that we have known each other in other lives and now we have come together in this one and so we are not really strangers."

"I think you have always been in my heart and at the back of my mind. From the moment I saw you I knew you were the one I had been looking for ever since I was old enough to know there was such a thing as love between a man and a woman."

"I want you to love me and I want to love you so that you will never be disappointed," Tarena murmured.

"Then we can only pray, Tarena, that one day it will happen. One day we will be free. What could happen I cannot say. I only know that I will dedicate my whole life to you, my darling, and perhaps one day we can really be together."

As he spoke, he looked back.

Tarena turned her head as well and saw that four soldiers on horseback were in the distance.

She looked at the Count questioningly and he said,

"It's quite all right, I told my men to come and look for me when it was time to return and they are just obeying my orders."

"You mean we must go back, Vladimir? Please, please can we ride like this another day?"

"It is something I would love more than anything else, but after tomorrow morning you will have a husband who would interfere."

"If he does, we must somehow evade him. I must see you, I must talk to you, I *must* be with you."

"My darling, my precious, Tarena, do you suppose I don't want to be with you every day and every night? But duty calls, and as Queen of Karlova you have to return. While I as Commander of the Palace Guard must look after you."

He did not say anything more, but set his horse into a brisk trot towards the soldiers now coming towards them.

There was nothing Tarena could do but ride back beside him.

*

When they reached the Palace, it was nearly nine o'clock and Tarena went into the dining room.

She had only just seated herself when the Comtesse came hurrying in.

"You did not tell me, Your Royal Highness," she blurted out, "that you were going riding and I have only just learnt of your return."

"It was such a lovely morning and I needed the exercise."

"I am supposed to know all Your Royal Highness's movements," the Comtesse replied in a disagreeable voice. "So I would be grateful if another time you would be kind enough to tell me, ma'am, what you are doing."

Tarena did not answer.

She was able to do so without seeming rude when at that moment her Uncle Richard came into the room.

She jumped up to kiss him and he remarked,

"I can see you have been riding. How very sensible of you! I wish you had told me, as I would have liked to accompany you."

"Why should we not go riding now?"

"I would love to do, but I am told I have to attend a meeting in the Palace this morning."

"A meeting?" Tarena queried.

"I thought you might have been told," the Earl said, "that the Prime Minister has called a special meeting to discuss the final organisation of the wedding and of course to take immense care of you and your bridegroom."

"Do you mean that they think we might be attacked on the way to Church?"

"I don't think that anyone has put it as bluntly as that, but naturally you will need protection and it would be a disaster if anything went wrong."

"Yes indeed!" Tarena exclaimed.

She was on the verge of saying more when Prince Igor appeared and the Earl and the Comtesse both rose respectfully to their feet.

"I have had breakfast," Prince Igor said. "I only stopped by to tell you that I am going to inspect the Palace and the stables. The Lord Chamberlain is anxious I should know my way about and appreciate what is here."

There was a note in his voice, when he said the last words, that made Tarena think he would not be impressed by anything.

Without saying a word to her, he then walked back towards the door.

Tarena suddenly became aware that the Comtesse's eyes were following him.

She wondered if what she was feeling for him was just admiration for a man of his position or perhaps she had other feelings for him.

Then she told herself that she was only imagining that there was any intimacy between them and she thought again how unpleasant he was and how much she hated him.

When breakfast was finished, the Count arrived to tell Tarena that there was a deputation of women who were waiting to see her and would she be kind enough to meet them?

"A deputation? Who are they and what do they require from me?"

"They are women who have campaigned for some time to improve the country's schools."

"Is it repairing or extending they need?"

"That is exactly the point," the Count smiled at her. "That is what they want to talk to you about. There are not many of them, but I have a distinct feeling that they will be very voluble on the subject."

Tarena laughed.

"Of course, I will see them just as soon as I have finished my breakfast."

"I would really love to go riding," the Earl said, "and I do want to before I leave."

Tarena gave a little cry.

"You are not thinking of leaving so soon, Uncle Richard?"

There was silence for a moment and then the Earl responded,

"You know, my dearest, that I have a great deal to do in England. Although I would like to stay here and help you with your problems, I must not neglect my own duties. You know better than anyone else that there are a great many of them."

Tarena sighed.

"I hate your going away, Uncle Richard."

"Perhaps I will be able to come back for a little while next year. I will certainly try."

"I suppose I will have to be content with that," Tarena commented, "but I will miss you very much."

She finished her coffee and rose from the table.

"I am ready to see these women now," she said to the Count.

"There is no hurry. They have settled themselves comfortably in one of the anterooms, and I think it's the very first time they have been brave enough to come to the Palace."

"Then I will listen to them and all their problems," asserted Tarena.

They left the breakfast room and when they were outside, she turned to the Count,

"If Uncle Richard is really going home, is there a gift I can give him to thank him for bringing me here? It was at a very awkward time for him, when he would have much preferred to stay at home."

"I think he would be very pleased if you gave him the Star of Karlova," the Count replied.

"What is that?" Tarena asked him.

"It is much the same as the Order of the Garter in England, which, as you know, is highly prized by anyone who receives it."

"Then that is what I must give Uncle Richard."

"Once you and Prince Igor are crowned," the Count said, "there are a number of people to whom you will have to award medals and titles."

Tarena gave a little cry.

"I have forgotten that a Queen could do that. Can I then give anyone a title like Uncle Richard's Earldom, if I think they deserve it?"

"Of course you can. I will give you a list of those who should be given a higher rank and those who deserve even the Star of Karlova."

"Can I therefore see what I am going to give to Uncle Richard?" Tarena asked.

"Of course. You will find a drawer of them in the library and also a book in which is written the names of everyone who has received the Star of Karlova in the last two hundred years."

"I will most certainly read it," Tarena smiled.

They then reached the room where the women were waiting for her and an equerry on duty outside hurried to open the door for her.

"Shall I see you at luncheon?" Tarena asked the Count.

"I am not certain. I will join you if I can. But as I have already told you, the meeting starts at eleven o'clock and I expect we will be talking for a long time."

Tarena was about to smile at him and then she remembered the meeting was to arrange her wedding.

Almost despite herself, she gave a little shudder.

As the equerry pulled open the door, she went in to listen to the women who were waiting for her.

*

It was well after eleven o'clock before they left.

When they finally said goodbye, all very grateful to her for her promise to help them, Tarena remembered that she wanted to find a Star of Karlova for her uncle.

She had already found her way to the library.

She thought while she was there she would choose some books to take to her bedroom so that she could read them in the night if she woke up and found it impossible to sleep.

It was then she suddenly remembered that it was likely her husband would expect to be in the bed beside her.

She knew that there were two large State rooms side by side and she would then make it clear from the very beginning that he slept in his room and she in hers.

She felt her whole being scream out at the thought of his coming near her and making her his wife.

Then, because she was frightened and upset by the very idea, she hurried into the library.

The drawer in which the Count said the Stars of Karlova were kept was in a large inlaid chest at the far end of the room.

When she opened the top drawer, she found what she was looking for.

There were a number of beautifully embroidered sashes and attached to each of them glittering brightly was a large Star of polished gold.

It was certainly a very distinctive medal and she could understand that any man who wore it would feel exceedingly proud.

Also in the drawer there was a sword with jewels in the hilt and Tarena knew it was for use at investitures to reward worthy Karlovan citizens.

She was handling the sword and thinking that the stones on the hilt must be very valuable, when she heard someone coming into the library.

"It will be safe for us to talk in here," she heard a man's voice say.

She was suddenly aware that it was Prince Igor who had spoken.

Because she had no wish to see him or for him to find that she was here, she moved quickly to the nearest window.

She slipped behind the long red velvet curtains.

She heard footsteps of men approaching and she prayed that Prince Igor would not discover her.

She had seen him once already today and that was quite enough and she had no wish to bandy words with him as they had done last night.

To her great relief she heard Prince Igor and the man with him stop behind one of the large bookcases in the centre of the room.

"Everything is arranged, Your Royal Highness," a man's voice said. "I've brought you the money that was promised to you. There's three million roubles in total, but the Russian Embassy in Alexandria will change it into any currency you require."

"Thank you," Prince Igor replied. "And what other plans have you made?"

"As soon as everyone retires tonight, you and the Comtesse will leave by the North door of the Palace. If you turn left and step down to the North gate, from which all the sentries will have been removed, you will find a carriage waiting to take you to the bay by the coast where a ship is waiting for you."

"That sounds excellent. Are you quite certain no one is aware of our arrangements?"

"Absolutely certain," the man replied. "Tomorrow morning it will be announced that you have disappeared and there will be chaos!"

Both laughed before the speaker went on,

"While the people are confused and angry that there will be no wedding, our troops will move in and it will be easy in the confusion for them to take over without any resistance or bloodshed."

"What about the Palace?" Prince Igor asked almost sharply.

"We've thought of that as well," the man replied. "Six bottles of drugged champagne will be given to the

125

Comtesse to hand out to the soldiers on guard, telling them to drink the health of the bride and bridegroom."

He gave a laugh before he added,

"I have never known a soldier yet who would not accept a drink whatever time of day or night it is offered to him!"

"That is true," Prince Igor agreed.

"It's all foolproof," the conspirator said. "And the Officers at Headquarters think that perhaps the Princess should meet with a regrettable accident, which will prevent her causing any trouble once we have taken over."

"Yes, that's a wise decision," Prince Igor answered. "She has caused enough difficulty and problems already by interfering with the Courts of Justice."

"I agree with Your Royal Highness," the man said, "and the sooner she is out of the way the better."

There was a rasping sound as if they were rising to their feet.

"Thank you for the money," Prince Igor muttered. "I am very grateful. And please tell your Leader that the Commander-in-Chief of the Army has co-operated fully. He will carry out your instructions to move most of his troops to the East side of the City while we move in on the West."

"I will see that he does so," was the answer.

As the man walked to the door, he said something in Russian that Tarena could not follow, but she thought it must have been some sort of joke because Prince Igor laughed before he followed him out of the library.

After they had gone, for a moment Tarena could only stand where she was, thinking that it could not have happened.

Surely she could not have overheard anything so appalling and despicable.

It seemed to her incredible that Prince Igor should actually conspire with the Russians and had accepted a huge bribe to leave everyone in total confusion while they moved in and took over Karlova.

For a while she felt that she must be dreaming and imagined the whole scenario.

Then she realised she must do something at once.

Nothing could be better in that everyone concerned with the wedding was just then involved in the meeting in the Throne Room.

'I have to tell them now,' she decided, 'and I have to make them believe me.'

She was afraid that they would not believe her.

Then she felt as if someone was guiding her and she was sure that it was her father.

After all, he had loved his people.

And he had kept them free from the Russians as long as he was alive.

Now she had to prevent them from carrying out this dreadful plot to take over the country and murder her.

She came from behind the curtain and saw that the drawer of the chest was still open.

As if again she was being guided, she took from it a glittering Star and sash as well as the sword.

Carrying them in her arms, she then walked slowly across the library.

She knew that she must be very careful not to be seen by Prince Igor if he was still about.

She opened the library door by a fraction and then looked round.

All she could see was the empty corridor.

Still holding onto the Star of Karlova and the sash in one hand and the big sword in the other, she hurried down the passage.

The Throne Room was some way from the library, but fortunately it was on the same side of the Palace and she did not have to go through the hall that was always filled with equerries and servants.

When she reached the door of the Throne Room, she saw that there were two sentries outside and an equerry who looked at her in surprise.

As he bowed, she demanded imperiously,

"I want to go into the meeting."

"I have my orders, Your Royal Highness, not to let anyone in until their discussions are finished."

Tarena smiled at the equerry.

"I think, as I have a very special present for my uncle, who will be leaving soon after the wedding, they will not be annoyed if I take up a little of their time."

The equerry smiled back, as he noticed what Tarena was carrying.

"Of course not, Your Royal Highness. I am sure he will be most honoured to receive the Star of Karlova."

"I know he will."

The equerry opened the door and she walked in.

The men were sitting at an oval table facing the Prime Minister, who was seated just below the throne.

When Tarena appeared, they stared for a moment and then slowly and reluctantly rose to their feet.

"You must forgive me, gentlemen" she began, "for interrupting you, but I have something of grave importance to tell you. But first, if you will allow me, I wish to give my uncle a special gift from Karlova and I hope he will wear it at my wedding before he returns to England."

Now, as she spoke, the men present were smiling at her and then the Prime Minister came in,

"But, of course, Your Royal Highness, we do all understand, and we are extremely grateful to the Earl of Grandbrooke for bringing you here."

Tarena walked up to the Prime Minister.

There was a small table in front of him on which she laid down the sword and the Star and sash.

As she stood to one side of the table, the Earl, as if he knew the procedure, rose and walked up to her.

Holding the glittering Star in her hand, Tarena said,

"The Earl of Grandbrooke, as Queen of Karlova, I bestow on you the Star of Karlova in gratitude for the help you have given to the people of my country. May the Star bless you for the rest of your life."

The Earl went down on one knee and she placed the sash with the Star over his shoulder.

Then he rose to his feet and turned round,

"I thank Your Royal Highness for this great honour, which I will always cherish."

He walked back to where he had been sitting.

Tarena then picked up the sword.

"Will Count Vladimir of Sazon come forward," she asked.

She saw the astonishment on the Count's face, but he obediently walked forward.

Without her saying anything, he knelt on one knee in front of her.

Tarena dubbed him on both shoulders and declared,

"On behalf of my country and to thank you for all you have done for our citizens, I now create you Prince Vladimir of Sazon."

There was an audible gasp from everyone present.

For a moment the Count looked up at her with a bewildered expression in his eyes and, as he rose to his feet and before he could speak, Tarena continued,

"Now I have a matter of great urgency to tell you all. It is something I am afraid you will find almost incredible."

Slowly, choosing her words carefully and speaking with a sincerity no one could question, she told them word for word everything she had just overheard.

She repeated the whole unbelievable story except the part about the Commander-in-Chief.

When she had finished, the Prime Minister said,

"I find it hard to believe what Her Royal Highness has just told us. Yet I know, and I am convinced as we all are, it is the truth and we must act accordingly."

"The first thing I will do," the Commander-in-Chief came in, "is to arrest Prince Igor and the Comtesse."

Tarena put up her hand.

"There is one thing yet I have not told you," she said. "It is that the Commander-in-Chief who has just spoken, has agreed to carry out orders from the Russians to take the majority of his troops to the East of the City while they intend to invade us from the West."

As she spoke, the Commander-in Chief had reached the door and, as he did so, he turned round and pulled a revolver from his belt.

He raised it and was aiming it directly at Tarena when the Count, who was still standing beside her, fired first.

He shot him full in the chest and he fell forward with a crash to the ground.

Everyone rose hastily to their feet and before they could say anything the new Prince Vladimir said sharply,

"He is dead, but it would be a mistake for anyone outside to be aware of it. Put his body out of sight until after the marriage has taken place tomorrow."

Those present all stared at him in astonishment.

Then he added,

"Now we know what our enemies are planning, we have to be absolutely certain that the Russian Army when it approaches us meets a very different reception from the one they are expecting."

Two of the younger Members of the Cabinet then picked up the Commander-in-Chief's body and carried it down the room and placed it under the platform.

There was silence until they returned to their seats.

In the meantime Tarena had sat down next to the Prime Minister with Prince Vladimir beside her.

When the two Members of the Cabinet were seated again, Prince Vladimir rose to his feet and asked,

"So what do you suggest we do next, gentlemen?"

Two or three men started speaking at the same time saying,

"Arrest Prince Igor and the Comtesse now."

"I have been thinking that over and I would advise that it would be a mistake," Prince Vladimir replied.

"Why?" the Prime Minister asked.

"Because then the Russians will know we are aware of what they have planned. However carefully we may keep their plot a secret, servants talk and someone, perhaps Prince Igor's valet, will find out that he is under arrest."

"I do see your point," a Minister said. "Let them go ahead and leave the country without them finding out that their plans have gone awry."

"What they intend is that we cancel the wedding, and that in itself will upset the people and give them an excellent excuse to take over the City."

There was silence for a moment and then Prince Vladimir turned and looked at Tarena.

"May I presume," he began, "that owing to Your Royal Highness's gracious action, we are now on equal terms. Therefore may I ask Your Royal Highness to do me the great honour of becoming my wife?"

"My answer," Tarena murmured, "is that it would make me very happy. I promise that you and I together will do everything in our power to make the people of Karlova safe and secure and as happy as we intend to be ourselves."

The men sitting round the table stared at her as if they could hardly believe what was happening.

Then, as if some of them guessed the truth, they gave a low cheer.

"Of course we are both surprised and delighted by what Your Royal Highness has said," the Prime Minister added. "But now comes a very difficult decision which we must make immediately. We must agree who is to take over the Army now that the Commander-in-Chief is no longer with us."

"I would be prepared to do so," Prince Vladimir said, "with the assistance of General Milan who I see is here at the moment."

"I will be very honoured," the General said, rising to his feet, "to serve under Your Royal Highness. I have always realised that you were right in so many initiatives you suggested, but you were ignored by the Commander-in-Chief."

"At least we know at what point the Russians will be approaching the City, no doubt overconfidently and that is where our Army will be waiting for them. Meanwhile our prime duty is to protect the Queen. I will arrange that my own special troops in whom I have complete trust, will guard the Palace and ourselves as we drive towards the Cathedral."

"When," the Prime Minister asked, "are we to let the people know that the marriage will take place, but there will be a different bridegroom?"

"Not until we have actually reached the Cathedral."

They looked surprised and Prince Vladimir added,

"We have found one Russian supporter here in our midst, in fact three, if we count in Prince Igor and the Comtesse. I think it would be a mistake if when we leave this room we breathe a single word to anyone of what has occurred. That includes your wives, your family and your staff. The Russians must not know anything until it is too late for them to change their plans."

He paused before he continued,

"If we all keep the secret, they will walk into a trap which will, I hope convince them painfully that, when Her Royal Highness and myself are on the throne, Karlova will never lose its independence!"

CHAPTER SEVEN

"Is it all right," the Prime Minister asked, "for us to leave now?"

"I believe," Prince Vladimir replied, "what really matters is that no one and I repeat no one, except ourselves, has the slightest idea of what has occurred in this room.

"I will see to everything that concerns the Palace and my future wife and we will then concentrate on the defence of the City."

The Prime Minister nodded.

Finally after some whispered conversation amongst themselves, they opened the door and moved into another part of the Palace.

Tarena slipped her hand into Prince Vladimir's.

"You were so right," she sighed. "God has helped us when we least expected it."

Vladimir smiled at her and then he realised that the last of the Cabinet had left the room.

The only man there besides himself was the Earl, and he walked over to Prince Vladimir.

"I cannot tell you," he said, "how happy it makes me to know that my niece will marry you and *not* Prince Igor."

"I hoped you would say that, my Lord."

"It is wonderful, Uncle Richard," Tarena enthused. "I love Vladimir and I know he loves me, which is the way I always wanted to be married."

"You have been a very brave and clever girl. Now I can go home in peace. I admit previously that I felt very worried about you."

"There is something I want to ask you," Vladimir said, "when are you leaving and how?"

"Actually I was not yet going to tell Tarena when I was going because I thought it would upset her, but I have arranged with the Captain of *The Royal Sovereign* that I will leave tomorrow after the marriage has taken place."

Vladimir made a sound that was almost a whoop of joy.

"*The Royal Sovereign!*" he exclaimed. "Where is she?"

"She should be coming into Port at any moment," the Earl replied. "I hope I was right in inviting the Captain to be present at the wedding."

"Of course you were right. He is the one man I want to see at this very moment."

"I will be very surprised if *The Royal Sovereign* is not in Port soon after luncheon," the Earl added.

"I expect our luncheon is ready now," Tarena came in.

Vladimir looked at the large clock on the wall.

"I hope you will forgive me, my darling, but I think I must skip luncheon as I have so much to see to. As it all concerns you, I know you will understand.

"And don't forget that no one must know I am not on my regular duty of guarding the Palace."

"What are you really going to do?" asked Tarena.

"Something which concerns you, my precious, and you will realise it is much more important than luncheon."

She smiled at her new Prince and she knew from the expression in his eyes that he wanted to kiss her.

It was what she wanted more than anything else, but it would be a mistake to do anything in the Palace that might seem unusual.

Vladimir hurried away, as Tarena slipped her arm through her uncle's.

"I am the luckiest and happiest girl in the whole world," she sighed.

"It is what you deserve, my dearest. You astonish me how brilliantly you have behaved since you came here. When I saw Prince Igor I was deeply worried."

"Not half as worried as I was, but now we need no longer concern ourselves with him or that evil Comtesse, thank goodness."

"But be careful, very careful," the Earl said, "not to say anything to arouse their suspicions."

They were very discreet at luncheon where the chef excelled himself in producing delicious dishes.

Prince Igor sat at one end of the table and Tarena at the other.

She was only afraid that he would see the happiness in her eyes and be aware that her heart was dancing.

Fortunately there were a good number of people at the luncheon, who come to see both Prince Igor and the Prime Minister. Having had to wait as the meeting had taken a long time, they had stayed on for luncheon.

When they left the table, Tarena was quite certain that Prince Igor had not the least idea how the situation had changed in the last few hours.

She went up to her bedroom.

It had been arranged she should try on her wedding gown after some alterations had been made to it.

She had felt indifferent until now how she looked as she had been quite certain that Prince Igor would hardly notice her anyway.

Now she wanted to look really lovely for the man she loved.

She took a great deal of care in fitting the gown and making sure that the train was long enough. And it had to be grand enough to impress everyone in the congregation as well as those outside who would merely see her walking up the steps and in through the West door.

"You will make a really lovely bride, Your Royal Highness," the dressmaker and her assistants chorused as they left.

"I hope you will all be there to see my happiness."

"Of course we will all be there," the dressmaker replied. "You will delight everyone who sees you and that will be everyone in the City."

"I only hope we don't get crushed to death," one of the assistants added.

Tarena could not help thinking that there might be more events happening that day than just her wedding.

The Russians would doubtless be banking on an announcement that the wedding would not take place and even when they learnt it was happening, they might attack the crowds who naturally would not be carrying weapons.

She felt herself shiver.

Then she thought that now Vladimir was in charge everything would be different.

She wondered where he had gone.

He had the enormous task of reversing the orders given by the Commander-in-Chief and making sure that the troops they did have were posted to face where the Russians were massing their forces.

'Please God help us,' Tarena prayed not once but a hundred times during the afternoon.

They had achieved so much so quickly, but she was terrified that at the last moment things would go wrong.

Perhaps she and Vladimir would not be married but taken prisoner.

When the dressmakers left, she went downstairs to see if there was any sign of Vladimir and, when she did so, she learnt from one of the equerries that Prince Igor had gone out.

But Vladimir had not yet returned.

Tarena went back to her boudoir and tried to read one of the books she had taken from the library.

But it was quite impossible not to keep going to the window to look out and see if there was anything unusual going on.

There was nothing.

Yet when she returned to her book, she found that she could not concentrate on even a word of it.

Then the door opened and to her delight, Vladimir came in.

She gave a cry of joy.

She would have run to him, but he put his finger to his lips, closing the door behind him.

She stopped dead and stood looking at him, her eyes wide and frightened.

"I have now come to tell you," he assured her, "that everything is arranged for your wedding tomorrow. You need not worry that anything has been forgotten."

With a tremendous effort, Tarena managed to reply,

"Thank you for letting me know, Vladimir."

"I thought you might be worried. Therefore I hope you will sleep peacefully and not feel concerned in any way."

He glanced at the clock and added,

"Dinner will be served in an hour's time. I hope you will excuse me from being present at dinner. I have, as you understand, arrangements to make for the troops under my command that specially concern the Palace."

"Yes – of course I understand – "

"The time of the marriage is now moved forward."

Tarena looked surprised.

"It was, as you know," he continued, "to have taken place at two o'clock, and the Reception would have been about four o'clock."

"How have things changed?"

"I have now arranged with the Archbishop that the wedding will be at eleven-thirty and the guests will be entertained not with just wedding cake and champagne, but with a full wedding breakfast."

Although he was speaking formally, Tarena could see that his eyes were filled with so much love and she had difficulty in concentrating on what he was saying.

"I want you to be ready to drive to the Cathedral at ten-thirty," Vladimir continued. "Of course I need not say to you, not to be late, because you are *never* late."

He accentuated the words.

It was then Tarena was quick enough to realise he was informing her that he intended to surprise the Russians by altering the time of the Service, hoping it would confuse them.

If they were not aware of it until the last moment, they could not put their cunning plan into operation.

That was, she was certain, to start fighting in the City Square after it was announced that Prince Igor had left and so the wedding had been cancelled, and then to seize control while the people were distracted by the news.

Now the people would not be confused, since the marriage would have already taken place and they could see the bride with the bridegroom, although an unexpected one, for themselves.

"I feel very sure," Tarena said aloud, "that your plans are excellent. I promise I will not be late."

Vladimir smiled.

It was with difficulty that Tarena prevented herself from running forward and throwing herself into his arms.

She realised that he was right in being careful about what they said as even the walls might have ears and there could be other traitors in the Palace.

"I sincerely hope that you will rest peacefully until tomorrow morning when I will see you again," Vladimir declared, as he bowed and left.

As he closed the door, Tarena said over and over again to herself,

'I love him, I love him. Oh, please God let us be together as we so long to be.'

Dinner was a heavy gloomy meal with Prince Igor grunting aggressively to anyone who tried to converse with him.

The Comtesse was obviously somewhat on edge and it was as if she was afraid something would prevent her from leaving with Prince Igor as secretly arranged.

With a tremendous effort, Tarena talked normally to her uncle who was on one side of her and the Minister for Foreign Affairs who was on the other.

They discussed in great detail every other country in Europe except the one they were in and the Earl made it much easier for her, simply by his presence.

When they went upstairs to bed soon after dinner was finished, the Earl kissed Tarena and said,

"You have behaved perfectly, my dearest, and I am very very proud of you."

"I only hope tomorrow will go forward as we pray it will," Tarena whispered.

"I don't think you need worry, but I am going to the Chapel now to say my prayers before I go to bed and I am quite certain that God will hear them."

"Pray very hard that I will be happy – "

"I have been doing that ever since we arrived here, dearest Tarena. I am sure now that my prayers have been answered."

Tarena hugged him, then went to her bedroom and left instructions that she was to be called early.

*

She slept fairly well considering all the excitements of the day.

She had her bath at half-past eight and there was breakfast for her alone in her boudoir.

She then started to dress and when she looked out of the window, she saw that it was a lovely day with the sun shining.

Everything was so quiet and normal and it seemed impossible that at any moment there might be gunfire and an attack by Russian soldiers.

Maids were waiting to help her into her wedding gown, which she was confident looked really beautiful and Regal.

When she added to it the tiara her uncle had lent her, she thought that Vladimir would indeed admire her.

That was what mattered most.

When she was ready, it was two minutes before half-past ten and she then proceeded very slowly down the stairs, followed by lady's-maids and footmen, lifting her train over the thick carpet.

Then she saw that her uncle was waiting for her in the hall and it was the first time she had seen him dressed for a grand public occasion not as a Priest but as the Earl of Grandbrooke.

He was proudly wearing the gold Star of Karlova she had given him and it combined well with the smartness of his attire.

"You look so beautiful, my dearest," he said to her.

She knew by the expression on the equerries' faces that they too thought she looked marvellous.

Then just as they were about to start walking down the steps outside to the carriage, one of the senior equerries whispered in the Earl's ear,

"We cannot find Prince Igor, my Lord. We have been to his room and his bed has not been slept in."

"Don't worry about it," the Earl replied. "It will all be explained to you later."

The equerry stepped back and the Earl and Tarena paraded down the steps.

There was already a small crowd waiting beside the four white horses that were to pull the 'Golden Coach' to the Cathedral.

The coach was open so that Tarena could be seen.

When she reached it, she saw ahead something she had not expected.

The crew of *The Royal Sovereign* were lined up to march in front of the Golden Coach and one of the Senior Officers was carrying a very large Union Jack.

Even as she looked at it, Tarena realised how clever Vladimir had been.

He was making sure not only to the people but to the Russians that Tarena had the full support and blessing of Queen Victoria of Great Britain.

When she and the Earl started off in the Golden Coach with the escort of British sailors and the huge Union Jack, she knew it would undoubtedly worry and bemuse the Russians.

She was therefore not surprised when, as a cheering crowd followed behind her carriage, there appeared to be no dissenters of any sort.

The Union Jack and the sailors reached the Square that was already filling with people who had arrived early.

As they did so, a large Regimental band outside the Cathedral burst into the National Anthem of Great Britain.

The sailors marching behind the flag came to a halt and stood rigidly to attention.

The Golden Coach stopped and the Earl rose to his feet and so did Tarena.

As the National Anthem finished, the Golden Coach moved on again to the bottom of the steps leading up to the West door of the Cathedral.

It was then the people in the crowd began to cheer and, if there was a protesting Russian amongst them, it was not possible to hear him.

The Earl climbed out of the carriage first.

When Tarena joined him, she turned round to wave to the people.

She had deliberately not hung the wedding veil over her face. Instead it fell down on either side of her face so that she could be seen clearly by everyone present.

The people cheered and cheered.

Then her uncle suggested,

"I think we should move up the steps now."

She was aware that he was afraid a Russian agent might take a shot at her.

At the same time she was absolutely certain that under the protection not only of Great Britain but of God Himself she would reach Vladimir in the Cathedral safely.

The Cathedral was packed.

Many of those living near the City had places kept for them, but it had been impossible to stop the more senior citizens from pushing their way into the Cathedral whether they had been invited or not.

What delighted Tarena, and she had not been aware of it, was that by some magical means of his own Vladimir had arranged for local children to be her bridesmaids.

They were all small and some were not more than three years of age and the oldest was only six.

Dressed in white and wearing wreaths of pink roses on their heads, they looked adorable.

As she processed up the aisle, they followed behind her, the older ones holding the younger ones by the hand.

When they reached the Chancel steps, Tarena saw that Vladimir was waiting for her.

He was looking smarter than she had ever seen him look before.

He was not wearing his Military uniform as she expected, but looked unbelievably distinguished in full morning dress with only a few decorations on his chest.

Standing beside Vladimir was the Captain of *The Royal Sovereign* and Tarena realised at once how astute it was of Vladimir to invite him to be his Best Man.

And he was also, for the occasion, representing Her Majesty, Queen Victoria.

The Service was shorter than Tarena had thought it would be and there again she was sure that it was Vladimir who had thought it would be a mistake for those outside to wait too long for the bride and bridegroom.

They knelt for the Blessing and to Tarena it was a very sacred moment.

Then the trumpets sounded out and the Coronation began.

The Archbishop then crowned Vladimir and Tarena as King and Queen of Karlova.

The whole congregation stood and applauded.

The organist played a stirring triumphal march as they walked down the aisle.

The West doors were flung wide open and the band below broke into the National Anthem of Karlova.

Tarena and Vladimir stood to attention.

It was then the people packed in the Square below began to sing the words of the Karlova National Anthem.

To Tarena it was very moving to hear their voices soaring up into the sky and to know they were singing to their new King and Queen.

Even before the last note sounded, they began to cheer and their cheers rang out louder than the trumpets.

They seemed to carry their delight and appreciation to Heaven itself.

Very slowly Tarena and Vladimir descended the steps, as small children ran in front of them strewing the way with rose petals.

When they had nearly reached the bottom step, they began again to wave to the cheering crowd.

It made a picture that most people watching felt they would always remember.

When Vladimir thought that they should move on, they stepped into the Golden Coach.

There were cheers and cries of 'good luck' and wishes for their future happiness all the way to the Palace.

Once again Vladimir had been wise.

A detachment of the Army with an Officer carrying the flag of Karlova stood on one side of the steps that led up to the Palace, on the other side stood the British sailors with the huge Union Jack held by an Officer from *The Royal Sovereign*.

It had been impossible for Tarena and Vladimir to say a word to each other as they were riding in the Golden Coach, because the noise from the crowd was deafening.

Finally they walked into the Palace and Tarena whispered to Vladimir,

"It was wonderful of you to think of asking the sailors from the Battleship to be with us. I am sure that is what prevented the Russians from interfering in any way.

"I think the main reason they did not interfere was simply that the marriage took place," he replied. "The people were so excited by seeing it that the Russians knew they would find no support from the rejoicing crowd."

"It was very very clever of you," Tarena insisted.

"It was you who made it possible, my darling, and I will begin to tell you later how much I love you."

As they went through the door, there was a crowd of Ministers and equerries and the Prime Minister to offer their congratulations.

They had gone ahead after leaving the Cathedral and were now waiting to enjoy the wedding feast the cooks had provided.

There was no doubt that the happiness and gaiety of those present was due to the Russians having turned away without firing a shot.

The fact that the wedding, which had been blessed by Queen Victoria had taken place, and that there was now a King and Queen of Karlova, meant that the Russians dared not risk a war against the British.

'We have won! We have won!' Tarena wanted to shout out, but it was impossible to speak to her husband when there were so many people eager to congratulate both of them.

It was now late in the evening when finally the last guests reluctantly left the Palace.

Already five times the bride and bridegroom had gone down the front steps and stood waving to the ever-increasing crowd below them.

They thanked them warmly from their hearts for their blessings and good wishes.

It was, of course, Tarena who thought of sending out sweets and biscuits for the children.

And it was King Vladimir who, at the end of the evening, said that there were to be free drinks in the public houses for all the men of Karlova.

He said he hoped that they would not bankrupt him with their thirst!

They all laughed.

At the same time it was something no Ruler had ever done before.

Finally Tarena was able to go upstairs to her own bedroom where her maids were waiting to take off all her jewels and her wedding gown.

"You looked so incredibly beautiful, Your Majesty, that I wanted to cry," one of the maids exclaimed.

"It has been such a wonderful day for me," Tarena answered. "I am happier than I have ever been in my whole life."

"We thinks as that's how Your Majesty looked," another maid said, "and how His Majesty looked too."

*

It was certainly how Vladimir looked when at last Tarena was alone and waiting for him in the big bed where so many Kings and Queens of Karlova had slept.

Tarena had been deeply touched when she went upstairs to find the whole room was decorated with white flowers and their scent filled the air.

Only Vladimir, she knew, could have thought of it.

Now, when he came in through the communicating-door, she held out both her arms.

He walked to the bed and stood looking down at her.

"Can this really be true?" he asked her. "Or am I dreaming?"

"It's true! It's true and *we have won!* Against all the odds the Russians have been defeated."

"I learnt tonight when I was undressing," Vladimir said, "that their troops are withdrawing, having suffered severe casualties when they unexpectedly met with firm resistance."

"I am certain now, Vladimir, that they will never come back."

"Not as long as we live and, of course, we will leave sons to take our place when we die."

Tarena drew in her breath.

"I love you," she sighed, "and I have no wish to die. I want to love you for ever."

"I will make certain you do!"

He took off his robe and then he blew out all the candles by the bed with the exception of one.

As he joined her, he thought that no one could look more beautiful or more ethereal.

"I have been waiting patiently for this moment for what seems a thousand centuries," he said. "Now at last, my darling, you are mine and no one can take you from me."

He spoke almost as if he challenged Heaven itself.

Tarena put her arms round his neck and drew him towards her.

"I love you, I adore you, Vladimir. Do you know that you have never yet kissed me?"

"That is something you will never say again."

Then his lips were on hers.

At first he kissed her tenderly and reverently as if she was infinitely precious and if he touched her, she might dissolve in his arms.

Then, as he felt her body melting into his, his kisses became more demanding, more passionate.

He knew because she was pure and untouched he must be very gentle with her.

At the same time the fire moving within them both was as bright as the silver moonlight streaming in through the window.

Both he and Tarena felt as if all the stars in the sky were twinkling within their breasts.

"I love you! God how I love you!" he murmured. "You are so perfect in every way. I know, my darling, no one will ever be as happy as we are tonight and we will be for the rest of our lives."

"And I so love and adore you, Vladimir. I thought we would never be together and I would die, never having known the feelings you are giving me now that are too marvellous to put into words."

"Then let me say it to you with kisses."

He kissed her until she felt as if he lifted her up into the sky and they were hugging the stars.

Then, as Vladimir made Tarena his, they both burst through the Gates of Paradise.

Their love which came from God, was blessed by God and was God Himself was theirs for ever into Eternity and beyond.